A HIGHLANDER'S HOPE

A MacKendimen Clan Novella

Possessed by the Highlander ♥
Taming The Highlander Rogue
The Highlander's Stolen Touch
At The Highlander's Mercy
The Forbidden Highlander
The Highlander's Dangerous Temptation ⚹
Yield to The Highlander
The Highlander's Inconvenient Bride
(Crossover with A HIGHLAND FEUDING series)

Related stories (same clan 500 years later)
The Earl's Secret+
Blame It On The Mistletoe♥****

THE KNIGHTS of BRITTANY STORIES:
A Night for Her Pleasure
The Conqueror's Lady
The Mercenary's Bride
His Enemy's Daughter

STAND-ALONE STORIES:
The Queen's Man
The Duchess's Next Husband
The Maid of Lorne
Kidnapping the Laird
What The Duchess Wants
Upon A Misty Skye
(previously in ONCE UPON A HAUNTED CASTLE⚹)
Across A Windswept Isle
A Traitor's Heart in BRANDYWINE BRIDES
The Storyteller – A Ghosts of Culloden
Moor Highland Novella
Tempted by Her Viking Enemy ♥
(part of Sons of Sigurd series)

**** RWA RITA® Finalist!!
♥ NJRW Golden Leaf Winner!!
⚹ USA TODAY Bestseller!!
∞RomReviews Best of 2011
+ Other Awards

A HIGHLANDER'S HOPE

A MacKendimen Clan Novella

A Highlander's Hope

ISBN: 978-1-949425-04-8

Book Cover Design: Dar Albert of Wicked Smart Designs
WickedSmartDesigns.com

Print Formatting: Nina Pierce (Nina@NinaPierce.com)

Chapter 1

Dunbarton Keep, Scotland
Late November, in the Year of Our Lord 1357

Iain MacKillop stared across the hall and watched as his nieces and nephews, brothers, and other kith and kin went about their usual tasks and routines. And with every passing second, he knew he was not needed.

The MacKillops had been at peace for years, their allies strong enough to deter any real trouble. As uncle of the chieftain and commander of all the MacKillop fighting men, he thought things had been quiet. Too quiet. With the worst of the winter coming soon, Iain could not imagine being here with all the squabbling and...children.

Having never been blessed with ones of his own before his wife passed, he now grew impatient around the young ones. 'Twas not that he disliked them; nay, it was rather that he'd wanted to have children too much.

Marry again, his nephew Jamie had said. Jamie had even offered to make arrangements for a suitable bride as befitted the uncle of the chieftain. Suitable bride, his arse! Jamie simply wanted to use him to cement some far-flung relationship, as his own father had done with Iain's first marriage. Now, though, Iain refused to be a pawn again.

As though thinking on Jamie's marriage plans had made him appear, Iain noticed his nephew approaching the table where Iain sat. Lifting the mug and pouring the last bit into his mouth, Iain stood and pushed the stool away, determined to avoid *this* again.

"Iain, stay a moment," Jamie said as he arrived next to Iain. "I have a matter to discuss with ye."

"Jamie, leave it be," he said. "I want no woman to wife now."

His nephew studied him in silence and nodded, before sitting down and drawing Iain down next to him. Holding up Iain's mug, he signaled his desire for ale to a passing maid. When a clean cup appeared filled with ale, his nephew drank deeply of it before speaking.

"I mean no disrespect to Elisabeth, uncle, when I urge you to remarry. I doubt she would want you to remain unhappy for the rest of your life."

"I am not unhappy," Iain replied. "And you do not know how Elisabeth would feel about it."

But Iain did. Elisabeth had begged him on her deathbed not to mourn her. To marry again. To have the children she could never give him with another. Iain's stomach soured at the memory.

"Fine," his nephew said. "Then I will put it plainly to you—I need you to strengthen our alliance with the

MacLarens. They have a daughter of marriageable age, and…"

Iain's expression must have changed without him realizing it, for his nephew stopped in the middle of his words. *Of marriageable age* meant a girl barely into womanhood. No matter that it was customary; as a man of more than two score years, he had no wish to take a near-child as his bride.

"Have I not served ye and our clan all my life, Jamie?"

he asked, already knowing the answer. "Have I not done everything asked of me by first yer father and then by ye?" Iain stood then, and his nephew raised his gaze to follow him. A curt nod was the only acknowledgement.

"Then if— *if* I decide to remarry, it will be my choice this time."

Iain strode the length of the hall and out of the keep.

Standing there in the cold November rain, he considered the issue that he'd thought was over and done. His stomach tightened as he remembered both Elisabeth's last wishes and his nephew's words and request. The truth in his heart was harder to accept than Jamie's suggested proposal.

He wanted to marry again. He craved the joys and simple pleasures that had existed between him and his wife.

And, aye, he wanted children more than anything in his heart or soul.

He kicked at a stone on the step next to his foot and sent it flying at the wall. Damn, but he wished they'd been blessed with children. Nay, his real wish was that Elisabeth yet lived and had born their bairns. Another stone flew against the wall.

It had been five years and the deepest pain had passed, but Iain would never forget her smile and her tender touch. And her soft ways and words.

Ye are no' a man to be alone, my love. Find someone who will make ye happy this time.

He'd argued with her then; for, though theirs had been an arranged marriage between strangers, their unexpected love had made him extremely happy. As was the usual way of things between them, even on her deathbed, she was right and spoke advice that was true. He did not like being alone. He would like to find someone. Mayhap he should allow Jamie his way in this? Let him make the arrangements?

The cold winds picked up then, whipping through the yard and around the stone keep. Buffeted by them, he wondered if mayhap Lisabeth was putting in her opinion about the matter? Nay, 'twas just the winds reminding him that winter would soon be upon them and the weather would make travel across the Highlands more difficult, if possible at all.

It had become his custom over these last years to visit Robbie Mathieson in Dunnedin over the darkest part of the winter. It was easier to celebrate Christ's Mass and the year's end there rather than here, where the memories of Elisabeth were so strong.

Make new memories, Iain. Love again. Live again.

Her words seemed to echo around him, and they

tormented him as they always did. But she did not mean to do that to him, for Elisabeth had given him permission to continue on without her. And he had.

Kicking the final stone there on the landing of the steps and watching it bounce off the wall, Iain took a deep breath and decided to leave this matter be for now. If he met a woman who stirred his desire for marriage, and not some child being thrust at him for the purpose of clan alliances, he would think on it once more.

Iain had to laugh aloud then, at the way that life and the fates sometimes conspired to show the folly of decisions and well-meaning plans. For in that moment, he realized that he *had* met someone who turned his thoughts in unusual directions. There was a woman whom he visited each time he made his way to Dunnedin. One who filled his thoughts every time he began his arrangements to visit the stronghold of the MacKendimen Clan. The woman who was the most inappropriate one in his life.

Robena MacKendimen.

He enjoyed spending time with her, and she seemed to welcome him there. But he was certain that she thought of him in a completely different way than he did about her. To her, he was a valued customer. To him, she was a splendid companion, even if she was the village harlot. He'd spent many hours, days even, in her company since Elisabeth's passing. She was intelligent, passionate, quick-witted, and…comfortable. She demanded nothing of him while offering so much to him.

As he sent off word to Robert that he would indeed

visit Dunnedin, as was his custom for the coming holidays and end-of-year festivities, Iain laughed at the preposterous idea that came to him then. Worse, the thought occurred to him several times over the next days before he left to journey there.

Robena MacKendimen as his wife.

His nephew and his other kin would die of apoplexy if he mentioned it. Mayhap he should, just to get Jamie to cease his badgering over it. Iain kept laughing aloud every time the thought struck him.

But by the time he rode from Dunbarton, the thought of it—of her—did not seem so nonsensical as before.

Dunnedin, Scotland

Robena heard the footsteps crunching up the path outside her cottage and stood. Though most men waited until night had fallen, some preferred their pleasure earlier in the day. She ran her fingers through her hair and shook out the wrinkles in her gown as she walked across the chamber. Putting on her best welcoming smile, she lifted the latch and tugged the door open to greet her guest.

"Robena," Rob Mathieson said as he nodded his head to her.

Of all the people—the men—who could be standing there, he was the last one she expected to see. Currently the tanist to the chieftain of the MacKendimen Clan, Rob had been her childhood friend before he'd been exiled by his natural father and fostered elsewhere. Almost five years ago, he'd been called back here and had, after a good amount of trouble and travails, found himself married to the Lady Anice and acknowledged by his father.

Happily married to the Lady Anice.

"What are ye doing here, Rob?" she asked, pulling the door closed behind her and stepping onto the path. In spite of her understanding with the lady, Robena wanted no gossip spreading about his presence here. The lady had turned to Robena in a time of difficulty, humiliation, and uncertainty, and Robena had counseled her in the ways of men and women. From all outward appearances, Robena's advice had helped and, in return, the lady had granted her entrance to the castle and keep.

"Iain sent word," Rob said. Holding out a piece of parchment, he explained. "He will visit here for the end of the year, until Hogmanay is done. I just thought ye would wish to ken?"

Robena tried not to smile as she gathered her hair up and tossed it over her shoulders. Iain was a friend of Rob's, and a favorite of hers as well. He paid well for her time, but more than that, she enjoyed that time with him.

"'Twould make things simpler if ye simply moved into the keep and stayed with him, ye ken?" Rob tucked the letter inside his tunic and shrugged. "After all, 'tis not a secret that he spends time with ye when he's here."

Men. She sighed. They always seemed to see things with a simple sense of clarity, while being able to ignore all the consequences and subtleties. Rob meant well, but she shook her head in reply.

"He must see to ye and the laird while I cannot be there. Ye ken how Struan feels about me being there when family is at table." In spite of the lady's acceptance, the laird would never allow it.

"I can speak to him." This was not the first time he'd offered to help in this matter.

"Nay, Rob." Robena shook her head again. "He is chieftain, and ye cannot naysay him simply to provide a whore for yer friend."

"Robena."

His blue eyes darkened in anger then, and he crossed his arms over his massive chest, making her feel very small next to him. It yet amazed her that at one time, they'd run as friends in this village, and she'd kept up with him and the others. Then, the changes that happened to make lads and lasses into men and women had forced them to acknowledge that they could not remain so.

And when her mother had died and Robena took over her place there, she'd never felt shame for it. Rob's wife Anice had made it clear that she accepted Robena's place in the clan, and so Robena was not mistreated or forced to do anything she did not wish to do. Truth be told, she had plenty of food, and warm clothing and a place to live.

Luckier than most women who served the baser needs of men.

"Rob, ye ken the way of it. How I live," she said, patting his arm now. "Tell Iain to visit when he can. I will be waiting for him." She turned to go back inside, for the November winds spoke of the coming winter and tore through her gown, chilling her. Rubbing her arms, she reached for the latch when Rob spoke again.

"He said he wants ye for his whole time here."

Her body, used to giving pleasure to men, reacted to those words. Iain was a generous man, and likewise a generous lover. He made certain she found pleasure in their every encounter. Not something a whore sought, but she appreciated his attentions to her needs. Now, at the thought of being only his for three or four weeks, her body warmed and throbbed. Robena shivered then, not at the cold winds but at the private heat that poured through her. She smiled as she met Rob's gaze then.

"'Tis fine. I will tell the others."

A few men visited her regularly each week, and she would let them know she had to see to The MacKillop's uncle during his visit. His honored position because of his connections would give him the exclusive right to her if he so desired, and he had asked for her during each of his visits here. That smile grew wider as she watched Rob nod and grunt something in reply before he turned and walked down her path towards the keep.

Iain was a handsome man, almost a score of years older than her own age, but as fit as a warrior could be. The man still held a position of authority and respect in the clan that was now led by his nephew. And he was a friend and mentor to Robbie. Neither his position nor his friendship made her feel the way she did about the man himself.

Robena closed the door and leaned against it, accepting the rush of heat that even the thought of Iain caused. Days and nights of passion lay ahead of her, and not even the fact that it should be an arrangement of business only could take away the knowledge that she wanted him. She wanted him there with her. She wanted to see and touch him.

She wanted Iain MacKillop more than 'twas good for a whore like her to want any man. It could not lead to anything good.

So, over the next days and nights, as she plied her trade with the men of Dunnedin, she tried not to pretend they were him. She tried to convince herself that she wanted him to arrive simply because she would be paid well, in gold, for his visits to her. Robena tried to keep the desire she felt for the man with the kind blue eyes and soft caresses under control.

She was a whore, and he was not for her. He could never be. She must learn to accept only what he gave her in exchange for her services. The uncle of the wealthy and powerful MacKillop Clan would never consider her worthy of anything more than the coin spent for her attentions.

She was a whore, and he was not for her.

Chapter 2

Iain accepted more ale from the passing servant and watched as Rob leaned in and whispered something to Anice. From the lady's blush, he comprehended the nature of Rob's comment to his wife. That his friend had found such happiness from such unhappy beginnings warmed Iain's heart. Even now, Rob was raising his half-brother's son as though the boy were his own, and it had brought out the best in a man raised without a father. From a few subtle signs that he recognized between them now, Iain suspected that an announcement about a new arrival would be coming soon.

As he inhaled the scent of the evergreens decorating the windows and hearth and other strategic places around the hall, Iain found himself reminded of the coming holyday and the celebrations planned for the end of the year. Anice's hall would glow with the light of many candles and lanterns when the dark of winter ruled outside. Each day the servants and the lady would add a few more sprigs of mistletoe and other greens to brighten the shadows. Though most of the feasting would wait until Twelfth Night, there would be enough spread over the next weeks and month for everyone to enjoy.

Glancing at the center chair at the table, he saw Struan MacKendimen also watching the pair, and wondered what the older man thought of the way things had gone. Struan had sent his natural son Rob away, to Iain's brother at Dunbarton, to keep his identity a secret from his clan and especially from the man Struan had cuckolded. But when Rob had returned here four years ago and saved Anice's and her son's lives, 'twas only a matter of time before their secrets were laid bare before all.

Soon, the lady excused herself from the table, and Rob moved to his side then. An attentive servant filled their cups and stepped away. Iain waited for the teasing to commence, for he was certain that his searching of the hall had been noticed by his friend. He could not seem to stem the growing sense of anticipation with each passing hour.

"She is not here," Rob said. "As ye already ken." Iain nodded and drank from the cup. "She refused my invitation." Iain drank again at his friend's words. "As ye also kenned she would."

"'Tis her way," he said.

"Iain, Anice has made her welcome here."

"More than most ladies would," Iain admitted. Most ladies would have had the village whore beaten or punished for trying to enter their hall. But here, the lady had befriended her. Iain knew part of their story, and Rob was at the center. He suspected that there was more he was not privy to about the matter.

"She likes ye, Iain. Have a care there, my friend."

The softly made declaration by Rob signified much to Iain. His friend had been not only friends with Robena, but also lovers at one time. When he had planned to leave Dunnedin and return to Dunbarton, Rob had asked Robena to accompany him…and to marry him. The offer, one made to give her the possibility of a new and different life, had been rejected long before Anice and Rob had overcome their challenges and the opposition of Struan MacKendimen. Still, though, in Iain's opinion, borne of many years of observing his friend, Rob continued a friendship with Robena that was unlike any Iain had witnessed before. So, Iain did not dismiss the warning in his words, either.

"It may surprise ye, but I like the lass," he answered back.

An exhalation was Rob's reply. His friend had not expected Iain's words and, candidly, he'd surprised himself by uttering them. They held a simple truth within them. He did like Robena. More than liked, he suspected, but he did not care to explain it to anyone. He would never hurt her.

He would have a care.

"Then why are ye still sitting here, man!" Rob said, smacking him on his back. "She waits for ye and the gates will close for the night soon. Make yer escape now."

Iain laughed loudly at Rob's permission to leave. He swallowed the remaining ale down in two mouthfuls before he stood. Why bother denying it? He wanted her.

He wanted to see her. He wanted to possess her and to pleasure her. His cock rose then. His body understood what was coming.

He tried to pace himself as he strode through the hall towards the door. Rob's boisterous laughter from the dais where he remained revealed his failure to do that. What would his friend think if he learned that Iain had made certain his horse was saddled just outside?

The guards waved him out and Iain followed the main road down from the keep into the village. Robena's cottage was near the other side of it, not far from the edge of Dunnedin. He urged the horse on as he saw the last turn ahead and soon he reached it, jumping to the ground before the horse had actually stopped.

The modest cottage appeared much as the others along this path did. A low fence surrounded it and Iain noticed the rope thrown over the gate—a signal that Robena was either engaged or out. If she was waiting for him, as Rob had said, then that rope was telling others to stay away. Iain led his horse around to the back and tied it there. He wanted to laugh as he walked to the door and raised his hand to knock, for he could feel the nervous anticipation growing.

Part of him, the very-hard cockstand beneath his plaid, needed him to barge in and take her until she could take no more. Part wanted to control the barbarian inside of him and allow some time to talk with her and reacquaint themselves to each other. Yet another part of him was completely and utterly confused over what to do. When the door opened, he gave up any hope of restraint and his expression must have shown it.

"I have been waiting for ye, laddie," Robena whispered as she reached out to him. Her smile was warm and welcoming as she grabbed hold of his cloak and pulled him closer, kissing him. He decided on his course as she opened her mouth to his tongue.

Iain wrapped his arms around her and savored the feel of her against him for a scant moment before backing her inside the cottage and kicking the door shut with his foot. She laughed against his mouth without ending the kiss. Somehow, she tugged his cloak off, loosened his belt— which allowed his plaid to drop to the floor— and had her hands under his shirt, on his skin, before they reached the pallet.

For a frantic moment, he drew away from her as he pulled the shirt over his head and she loosened the ties on her gown. Iain watched the fabric slide over her ample breasts and down over her curving hips, revealing the dark thatch of hair between her legs. He reached out to touch her there, sliding two impatient fingers deep within as she arched against them. His gaze never moved from hers and Iain felt his cock harden even more as the wetness covered his fingers.

He thrust a little deeper, swirling his fingers as they discovered a sensitive spot that made her gasp. Her eyes took on a dreamy appearance as he rubbed harder and faster, sliding in and then rubbing along her cleft. Allowing him his way, Robena breathed in shallow gasps as he felt her arousal grow. Then, she grasped his cock in her hand, encircling it and stroking it. Now it was his turn to hiss in pleasure. When she moved out of his grasp and fell to her knees before him, he shook his head.

"Nay, lass," he said, taking hold of her shoulders and bringing her to stand. "There's no time for that now."

He waited for any hesitation in her gaze before he lifted her to her feet, guided her legs around his waist, and entered her in one swift thrust. The sigh she released as he filled her warmed his old heart. Iain could not describe the way it felt to be so deeply inside her body. Her nipples tightened and pressed against his chest.

Robena slid her hands around his shoulders and loosened his hair from its leather tie, entangling her fingers as she grabbed hold of it. She lifted herself up, sliding along his length, and then pushed back down while meeting his gaze again. The second time, he aided her with his hands under her arse. The third time, the need to make her scream out in release overwhelmed him, so he dropped to his knees, taking her with him, and then guided her to lie back on the pallet.

"More," she whispered, arching her hips and taking him deeper still. "More, Iain."

Everything blurred then into a fury of passion as he touched and took her. In spite of thinking that his release would be a quick one this first time, Iain's seed did not spill until he had made her scream out three times in pleasure. When she tightened around his cock that last time, he let go with a roar.

For a time, the blood rushed in his ears and every sound seemed magnified. His breathing and hers echoed within him. The creaking of his boots as he shifted to keep most of his weight off her. The long, soft sigh she released as she stroked his back.

"There was no need to rush so, Iain," she whispered, merriment filling her voice. "Ye could have taken off yer boots first." He laughed in reply, falling on his back and tucking her to his side.

"Ye do that to me, lass," he admitted. "I thought of little else on my journey here, or through what felt like the longest meal ever consumed."

Robena would be the first to admit that his words made her feel as warm inside as his attentions had. The look in his dark blue eyes told her he wanted her for she'd seen the desire there when she opened the door. It did not take a whore's knowledge to recognize the readiness of his flesh beneath his plaid. She stroked his arm now, even while she rubbed her leg against his leg. And against his boots.

Sitting up, she shimmied down along his body and loosened his boots. Unconcerned with her lack of clothing, she knelt at his feet and tugged them off, tossing them into the same pile that his plaid and shirt had made when they'd hit the floor. Grabbing up a few more blankets, she shook them over him and then joined him once more. The heat pouring off his body more than made up for the lack of clothing in the coolness of the cottage.

"Have ye eaten, lass?" he asked. She settled against him, sliding her leg over his.

"Aye. But there is stew and bread and cheese, if ye wish it," she said. The lady had sent over food and ale in anticipation that Iain would spend his nights with her. She could send for more, or go herself if needed, for Iain was an honored guest here in Dunnedin.

"I think I ate," he said. His laughter rumbled deep in his chest and she could feel it under her hand. "I told ye, I wasna thinking about the food."

Robena pushed herself up, climbing from the warmth of the blankets and him to ready some food for him. It took little time to scoop some stew into a bowl and return to him.

"Would ye like to sit at table?" she asked, nodding to the table and stools in the corner of the cottage near the hearth.

"Nay," he said, sitting up and crossing his legs. "I will take that."

Robena handed him the bowl and poured ale into two cups before sitting with him on the pallet. Watching the way he shoveled the thick, savory stew into his mouth with barely a pause, she realized he had rushed here to be with her.

"So, tell me of the villagers," he said, nodding at her to talk.

She fell into her stories easily, telling Iain about the people who lived here and what had happened since his last visit almost four months before. That he knew them and seemed interested in them was something that Robena liked about him. He could have remained a visitor, an honored one at that, and yet he'd become part of the town. 'Twas not unusual for Iain to work with Rob's warriors, or even to spend time working in the village as *needed.*

"Moira and Pol are discussing marriage," she began.

"Again?" He laughed, and she loved the sound of it.

"I think it has become their end-of-year ritual. As the dark of winter, and Christ's Mass, approach, he asks once more. She thinks on it through Hogmanay and the new year, as he tries to convince her to say aye. By spring, they forget and continue on as they have been for years." The blacksmith and the healer had two daughters together and were inseparable, so the whole village loved to watch his yearly campaign. Wooing at its best.

Robena watched the way Iain's eyes sparkled and how easily he was moved to laughter. He was almost a score of years older than her, but he was yet filled with the vigor and enjoyment of life. He asked about this one or that, and she gave him bits about each one until he finished eating and she finished telling him about the changes and happenings in Dunnedin since his last visit. But mostly, she just looked her fill at the breadth of his chest and the masculine angles of his face.

It took a few moments of silence before she realized he'd emptied his bowl and cup and was sitting and staring back at her. She stood and reached for those and put them in the bucket near the door to be washed…later, from the desire that filled his gaze now.

"'Tis not late enough to sleep," she said as she watched him stand. His male flesh did as well.

"Aye, 'tis not." Instead of reaching for her, he walked past her and picked up her gown and shift. "And there will be plenty of time for that," he said, understanding her expectation. "I need to walk a bit after riding for these last days. Do ye mind?" He held out her garments to her.

"'Tis yer time to do as ye please, Iain." And his coin. She would naysay him not at all during his time here.

His gaze darkened, and a flash of something moved over his expression. She, who could read men and their needs and wants, was mystified, for it was either anger or disappointment. At her? What had she said to cause it? Then it was gone, and he nodded at the clothing in her hands.

"Join me?" He'd surprised her, which startled her even more.

Robena nodded and got dressed quickly. No matter her haste, she could not help but watch him, trying to understand his mood, his needs.

Men were creatures of habit, and she'd learned early on to be mindful of those habits in her customers. Men also appreciated her attention to the details, so they did not have to repeat themselves. They liked it when she acted on their preferences without them having to ask. Though there were those who liked the ordering part of things, most enjoyed the feeling that they were special enough to remember. And they paid well for that from her.

Iain paid her well for that. But this was not his habit to do. Usually, on shorter visits, he spent most of their time together on that pallet, barely pausing to eat or sleep. On his longer visits, over the dark days and nights of midwinter, he slept here, and spent most of his days with Robbie and the others.

Something was different now. Not in a bad way, but

in a way that set her senses off. Watching him, he seemed to be thinking on some matter that made him quieter than usual. He lifted her cloak from the peg by the door and held it for her. When she tied it on, he lifted the latch and waited for her to go first.

The night air swirled around them, cold but not damp. Winter was nigh, and they but waited for the first storm of the season to strike. She lifted her head and inhaled deeply, enjoying the fresh coldness of it. A nigh-to-full moon lit the ground and made it easier to see their way. Though she could walk the village paths in sheer darkness, he did not know his way around as well.

"Do you have a place in mind to go?" she asked.

"Nay," he said, holding out his hand to her. "Just around."

She took his hand and he pulled her closer, tucking her into his side, though she was used to walking without touching him. Admittedly, in the chill of the night, his nearness warmed her. He shortened his longer paces to fit hers and they made their way along the path through the village.

Since they encountered no one at this time of night, Robena wondered if that was the reason why he touched her so outside her cottage. Everyone in the village knew of his visits, so it would surprise no one, but he also did not make it his custom to do this. She glanced at their joined hands and wondered what to make of it. He pulled her to a stop then and turned her to face him. Pushing the hood of her cloak back, he grabbed her shoulders and lifted her face to his.

And kissed her over and over until she was breathless.

When he lifted his head and gazed down at her, there was something there in his eyes she'd not seen before. An emotion that had no place between a man and his whore. Something that would muck up everything between them, if she was correct about what she saw there.

Terrified at the very thought, she did the only thing she knew to do—she wrapped her arms around him and kissed him back.

Chapter 3

He'd frightened her, and he knew it. As he watched the fear enter her eyes, Iain realized his mistake at once. But things had changed for him—for them—and he'd no way of explaining it to her yet.

She'd expected he was there for the sex, and she knew how to do that. She was well familiar with the ways in which to please him. 'Twas the change from their usual patterns of things that concerned—nay, terrified—her now.

He slipped his hands around her hips and held her there. Kissing her was no hardship, and, if it allowed her to regain her footing in this situation between them, so be it. Holding her this close, she could feel the erection that had not diminished at all since she'd witnessed its rising. Her tongue was skillful at tasting his mouth. He tilted his head and let her have her way. Steam rose from their mouths and drifted into the cold of the night as they breathed around the sparring of their tongues.

Finally, he lifted his mouth from hers and let her slide down until her feet touched the ground, enjoying every second of the way her body's soft curves caressed him.

There would be time enough to enjoy the pleasures she offered him later. Now he truly did need to walk off the hours of being on a horse. His bones were not as young as they and he used to be, in spite of the vigor this young woman inspired in him.

Iain straightened her cloak and put his arm around her shoulders, drawing her in close against the worst of the cold before walking once more. They spoke not as they walked down the main road of the village and then off towards the loch on one of the paths. Every step eased the stiffness in his legs. He remembered enough of the layout of the village to guide them back to her cottage.

"Ye have been quiet, lass," he said as they approached her gate. "Nothing to say?" He lifted the latch once more, and lifted his arm from her shoulders, allowing her to walk up the path.

"I was not certain what ye wanted of me, Iain," she said. Ah, as he'd suspected—she feared the unexpected in the men with whom she…dealt.

She lifted the door's latch and pushed it open. The warmth inside made him realize how cold the weather was becoming, and how close the winter storms were. He watched as she crossed to the hearth before loosening her cloak.

"Just yer companionship on my walk." He took the cloak and hung it back next to the door. "I am feeling old and worn."

The way she lifted one brow in reply was something Iain would always remember and treasure. For in that one slight raised brow, she both accepted and denied the possibility that he aged.

"Ye could not prove that by me," she said, turning to stoke the fire in the hearth. He strode to her and wrapped his arms around her from behind, kissing her neck.

"Ye have a way of making me feel as young as ye are." 'Twas the truth of it. With her, though there was nothing to prove, he did feel much the way he used to in the early days of his marriage to Elisabeth. Randy. Full of life.

Always ready. A surge beneath his belt made him laugh.

"Ah, *that* young, then?" she asked, pressing against him.

He enjoyed the wordplay with her, almost as much as the bedplay. Iain had a sense that much of it came easily to her, and yet he could feel a genuine sentiment behind those two acts. Or did he mistake her interest in him?

Was he only a customer to her after all?

He would not be the first man to be fooled by a whore's feigned attentions. And not the first old fool excited by a young, comely woman. Was that all there was between them? As though to confirm his doubts, Robena turned in his embrace and slid her hands between them.

She met his stare as her hands covered his erection. The layers of woolen plaid and linen shirt mattered not as she stroked and massaged his length. When she gathered the plaid and slipped her hands beneath, touching his cock, he surged once more in her grasp. He clenched his jaws closed but did not move his gaze from hers as she drove him to madness. As always, she knew the point of no turning back, and released him then.

He allowed her to guide him back to the pallet and watched as she undressed him and then pushed him onto the bed's surface. The blankets were still as they'd left them from their last encounter. When she would have taken hold of him once more and drawn his release with her hot mouth, clothed and distant, he shook his head at her.

"Take me, Robena. As ye will." He smiled then, returning the wicked one that lay on her lips. "If ye want."

"Aye, Iain," she whispered as she unlaced and dropped her gown and shift once more. He looked his fill as she knelt at his side. "I want ye. God Almighty, forgive me, but I want ye."

He had only moments to consider those strange words before she began to ply her ministrations. Minutes or hours later, he knew not which, they lay sprawled across the pallet together and Robbie's words came back to him.

She likes ye, Iain. Have a care there.

Mayhap he did not need to doubt the affections she showed him? Mayhap her words about wanting him *were* true? She whispered then in her sleep, and he tried to understand what she said. He heard his name and smiled. There was time to sort this out. Time to discover if the daft and, aye, *dangerous* idea that had plagued him over these last weeks and on his journey could be possible.

She likes ye, Iain. And she wanted him, too.

Promising things to know.

And weeks to determine what the fates planned for him.

The soft knock woke her. Forcing her eyes to open against the brightness, Robena noticed several things almost at once. If her eyes did not deceive her, the sun had been up for some time, and it was later in the morning than she usually rose. In spite of the probable time, Iain snored loudly at her side, sleeping soundly through the sun's rising *and* the knock at the door. Iain gave no sign of leaving.

Creeping from the pallet, she pulled on her gown as quietly as she could before opening the door a scant inch to see who waited there.

"Mam says she needs ye, Robena," a soft voice whispered from outside. Daring to push the door a bit more, she found the midwife's youngest daughter standing there. "Anna's and Margaret's bairns are coming and Mam needs to be with Anna." Two young women giving birth to their first bairns, and the midwife could only be with one—the one who needed her skills more.

Robena glanced over her shoulder to where Iain slept. Though he'd never remained here after a night together, he showed no sign of waking or leaving now. Torn between angering him or ignoring this call for her help, Robena nodded at the lass.

"I will go to Margaret's," she said. The girl scampered off down the path, returning to her mother with word of Robena's attendance where she was needed.

Closing the door as quietly as she could manage, Robena picked up her clothing and dressed. Gathering her hair up, she wove a braid to keep it under control during the coming hours. Looking around, she knew there was nothing more to bring. If the birth went as it should, only water and cloths would be needed.

A snore echoed, reminding her of the man in her bed.

Deciding not to wake him, she grabbed her cloak and left quickly. She made her way through the village and down the path to Margaret's cottage, and found the young woman inside with her husband Conran and her sister-by-marriage. Nodding at those two, she untied her cloak.

"How do ye fare, Margaret?" she asked, tossing her cloak over a chair and walking towards her. One glance at the young woman told Robena what she needed to know.

"Torra, how long has it been?"

"Since last night after supper," Conran offered first. His nervous gaze flitted from his wife to Robena to his sister, and then back to Margaret.

"Conran, this may take time," Robena said, taking hold of the man's arm. "Mayhap ye should go about yer business and we can send word when it is time?"

"If ye think…" The man's expression showed both fear and relief at her words. "Margaret?"

"Aye, Conran. Go." Margaret gave a trembling smile

to her husband and nodded at the door. "Robena will see to things here."

Conran, bless him, rushed to Margaret and kissed her before leaving. His whispered words of love were loud enough for them all to hear and made Robena's eyes water with emotion. Then the young man rushed out so quickly that they just stared at the door for a moment before laughing.

"Will it take long?" Margaret asked as Robena went to her and helped her to the pallet.

"Nay, but I thought it best to make Conran think so." A hand on Margaret's belly warned her of the contraction within and told her of the strength and duration of it. "I suspect this bairn will be born before midday." Margaret frowned and glanced at Torra, who shrugged in reply. "What is the matter?"

"Robena, 'tis past midday now. Mayhap ye meant sunset?"

Stunned, she sat back on her heels and shook her head. "It canna be. I never sleep past sunrise." Now Margaret and Torra smiled knowingly at her.

They knew Iain had visited her last night. That he was there in her cottage even now.

"Sometimes our work wears us out," Torra said, winking at Robena. "And a fine man like that would certainly do so." Torra was a young widow who had lost her husband a year or so ago. And, according to the praise Torra expressed for him, he had been a fine man.

"Come now," she warned, easing Margaret onto her side. "Neither of ye should be lying to me about the time of day."

It simply could not be as late as they said. But, as the hours passed and Margaret's bairn pushed his way into the world, the growing shadows outside bore out the truth of their words. Only when the mother and bairn had been seen to did she allow herself to worry over Iain's reaction to waking in her empty cottage alone.

Now, as night approached, Robena wondered if he had returned to the keep or yet remained in the village.

"I will go fetch Conran," she said, once the bairn was nursing well at his mother's breast. Stretching to ease the tightness in her back, she grabbed her cloak. "I will send word to Daracha of the bairn and return in the morn to see ye."

"I will see to them," Torra promised.

Robena did not bother to put her cloak on then, for the hours in the overly heated cottage had left her hot and sweating. A short time in the cold would be a relief. With a farewell nod to the women, she pushed open the door and found Iain there with Conran.

"See, Conran? She smiles, so all must be well," Iain said. She did not realize she'd smiled, but she had.

"Aye, all is well, Conran. Go and see yer wife and… child," she said, not wishing to spoil Margaret's chance to tell her husband of their son. Robena waited until Conran had entered before looking at Iain. His expression told her little about his disposition at this moment.

"I…"

"Ye didna tell me about this when ye told me all the other news of the villagers," he said. And still she could not read his intent or his temperament.

She shivered as the cold air seeped through the sweaty dampness in her gown. He lifted her cloak from her arm and tossed it around her shoulders. He tugged the edges of it together and then pulled her to him. Iain studied her face before leaning down and kissing her softly on her mouth. The rumbling in her belly was loud enough for them both to hear. His smile, broad and genuine, made something within her warm and tingly.

"Have ye not eaten, lass?" he asked as he eased his hold on her cloak.

"I was busy with other matters, and there never seemed a good time to," she explained. "I beg yer pardon for leaving ye there without a word." He placed the pad of his finger over her lips before she could say anything else.

"Come," he said, taking her hand and leading her to his horse. "Rob said to bring ye in—into the kitchen, if ye protest entering the hall—for a meal."

Too exhausted to fight him, she allowed him to mount and to lift her up behind him. She might have slept along the way; up the road, then up the hill into the keep. The gates would be closing soon, so she could not tarry here. When they stopped, Iain handed her down first and then climbed down. A boy, alerted by some watchful guard, stood ready to take care of Iain's horse.

She did not remember much about the food, except that it was hot and well-seasoned and plentiful. Iain sat across from her, pushing chunks of bread to her in between spoonfuls of the thick soup. A cup of mulled cider was filled each time she took a sip. Iain played the servant well, but she felt guilty that he did. He was paying her for services, not the other way around, and she had failed to see to his needs.

And she would have, except that the weariness took over as the thrill of assisting in a successful birth waned. The next thing she saw was the sunlight peeking through the wooden shutter of the window in…Iain's chamber!

The bed was empty but for her, and she pushed the bedcovers back, sliding from the warm cocoon into the chill air of the morning. If there had been a fire to keep the cold at bay, it had long ago gone out, and now she could see her breath in the air before her. She gasped as her bare feet touched the frigid stone floor. At the sound of the door opening, she jumped back into the bed and pulled the blankets to her chin.

Iain opened the door wide and allowed a stream of servants to come into the chamber. Some carried food and drink. Some carried buckets of steaming water, and others brought drying cloths and soap and other necessary things for a bath. When she would have protested, he glared at her.

"Say not a word, Robena," he ordered, and his stern tone caught the attention of the servants, too. "Finish," he said to them.

It took but a few minutes before a meal was set on the table in the corner, the fire was fed and stoked, and a bath sat steaming near the fire. She knew that Anice's household was efficient and thorough, but this gave her a new appreciation of them. When the last of them left,

Iain closed the door and dropped the latch. Crossing his arms over his chest, he looked to her.

"Eat or bathe first?" His voice was deep, almost a growl, as he asked her to choose.

"What? Iain, I canna…" He covered the distance between the door and bed in three long strides and stood over her now. She knew what he was trying to do—frighten her into doing his bidding in this—yet she did not fear his strength in that way.

"Eat or bathe, Robena?" he asked once more. "Or should I decide for ye?"

Before she could utter a sound, he tugged the bedcovers from her grip, tossed them aside, and lifted her in his arms. His body warmed her as he walked away from the bed towards the tub, his intent clear to her now. Even knowing how it would feel, she could not prevent the sigh of pure bliss that escaped as he lowered her into the heated water. She did not move, not wishing to get him wet, as he placed her there and stood back.

The warmth surrounded her, easing the tightness in her back and legs. She may have sighed again, or it may have been a moan, but his laughter told her the sound had been heard. She allowed herself a short while to enjoy it, a very short while, before remembering the reason she was here.

"Would ye like to join me?" she asked. "The tub could hold us both."

When he tugged his shirt off, she thought he would do just that—climb in with her. Instead, he knelt at the end of the very large wooden tub where her head rested and lifted the jar of soap to the edge.

"Wet yer hair, lass."

She glanced at him once more over her shoulder before complying. His strong fingers spread the soap into her hair, and she closed her eyes as he not only washed her hair but also rubbed her sore shoulders and neck.

When his hands slipped over her skin and nearer to her breasts, she felt the tips tighten in the hot water. The circling motions moved lower onto her breasts and she arched, baring and offering them to him. As his actions remained those of simply bathing her, she wondered at it. He pushed her forward and twisted the length of her hair around his hand, then sculpted it on top of her head to keep it out of the water.

Once again, with strong and gentle fingers, he scrubbed her back, pressing on the places that ached the most.

"If yer going to continue in this, lass, ye need to have a care for yerself," he said softly.

Robena completely misunderstood his words. Iain could tell from the way she turned to stare at him. Shock and disbelief filled her eyes, darkening the usual bright green to something like the color of the forests at dusk. She thought him advising her on being a whore. Iain laughed, resting his elbows on the edge of the tub now, as understanding entered her gaze.

"Oh," she said with a shrug. "'Tis a bit harder bringing a bairn into the world than bringing a man to his pleasure." His flesh responded to her words and she glanced over the tub at the tenting of his plaid. "Just so."

Iain ignored the call of his body and moved to the side of the tub, holding out his hand for her to lift a leg into his grasp. Spreading the soap over her thigh, over her knee, down to her shapely ankle, he knew he could have her the moment he indicated it was his wish to do so. Mayhap that was why the frantic need that had assailed him for weeks was now tempered? Having her at hand made it easier to control his desire, because she *was* his—his indeed for the taking.

"When did you begin helping with births?" He did not miss an arousing view of the curls between her legs as she moved the one leg back into the water and held the other up to him.

"Just after yer last visit here in the summer," she explained as she allowed him to have his way. "Moira is taken with her duties as healer and seeing to her own wee uns." Moira's lasses had just four or five years to them and were a handful, he knew. "Daracha needs help tending to some of the women, so I help." She reached out and placed her hand on his. "I do beg yer pardon for leaving ye without word this morn. I ken ye are paying that I am yers to serve ye as ye wish—"

"Robena." He could not help that his voice came out harshly at first. "Surely ye ken me better than that?" He rinsed the soap from his hands and stood, saddened somehow that she would think him so uncaring about the travails of a woman giving birth. Or any other reason that she thought important enough to leave her cottage, whether on a cold winter's morn or whenever. "If ye think that I hold my comfort higher than tending to a woman in childbirth, then…" Iain let his words trail off as he grabbed up a drying cloth and wiped the water off his skin.

Women died in childbirth—it was the most dangerous thing a woman could do. It was something he had always feared as a possibility of Elisabeth carrying his child. His own sister had, and so many others among his kith and kin. The splashing water drew his attention back to the tub and the woman in it.

"I was surprised that ye were gone, that is all. Worried a bit about what could be so important to ye, if truth be told." He walked back closer and unraveled her hair. A bucket stood near the fire for a final rinsing. "Then Anice told me that ye had been called to Conlan's wife." He held out his hand to help her stand then. She turned her back to him and he poured the hot water slowly over her head, watching as it sluiced over every inch of her skin. "So I waited, thinking ye would be hungry or tired."

Robena turned then and wiped the water from her eyes. She smiled and nodded.

"Aye, I was both of those." He shook out the larger drying cloth and held it out to her. As she wrapped it around her, he did the same with a smaller one around her hair.

"I thank ye for seeing to me, last night and now with this." She tucked in the one cloth and rubbed her hair with the other. "This was a wonderful and unexpected gift."

She stepped up to him, stood on her toes, and kissed him. Full of warmth, he wished he had more time to accept the promise in the touch of her mouth, the way she rested her hand on his hip. If it would convince her to stay here, he would promise her a bath daily.

He, or rather his randy flesh, had just decided that his presence would not be missed in the yard where the men were training, when a loud knock on the door warned him otherwise. Rob gave that scant warning before he pulled the door open and yelled. Though Iain knew she was comfortable in her nakedness, he stepped between her and the door, not wishing to expose her to Rob's gaze now.

"Come on, Iain. Ye have had enough time to see to this," Rob called out. "The weather is holding for now, so ye canna avoid being beaten into the ground any longer." Iain dropped his head back and laughed at the words that were both a challenge and an insult at the same time.

"Have a care, pup," Iain warned his friend. "I may have more years than ye, but I also have more years of practice in teaching young ones a lesson."

As he glanced over his shoulder at her, Robena let the towel around her hair drop, and Iain was tempted, very tempted, to slam the door and remain with her. With a wicked gleam in her lovely blue eyes, she smiled and nodded.

"I think he needs a lesson about disrespect, Iain," she said.

Cursing, Rob pulled the door closed and left them, his taunting message delivered.

"Iain, I am very grateful for ye seeing to my needs, both last night and in arranging this bath," she said.

He had enjoyed taking care of her, for she gave him little opportunity to do so. After he'd kept her awake for most of the night, she'd gone off and helped a woman give birth, spending almost the entire day assisting Conlan's wife. From what Conlan had revealed, she'd done this for almost a dozen women in the village over the last few months. For a woman who'd never given birth herself, he thought it both brave and selfless of her.

If he were honest about his motives, Iain would have to admit that tending to her felt very good to him.

Though most of his kith and kin thought that he missed being taken care of by a wife, and indeed he did, Iain missed being able to take care of someone just as much.

"I will be waiting for ye after supper," she promised after he'd dressed and opened the door. He nodded and walked out to beat Rob to a pulp as he deserved.

That realization—that he missed tending to a woman's needs—made so many things clear to him, and he thought on little else but that as he showed Rob no mercy that day in training. Well, that and the woman who would be waiting for his arrival this night.

Chapter 4

It took her but a few moments to realize the first of her problems—she had no clothes.

After Iain left, wearing a very strange expression on his face, Robena had searched his chamber for her gown, tunic, stockings, and shoes. As she searched the cupboard in the corner, she wondered if this was a plan on his part to keep her there. That brought a smile to her own face, for it was a demonstration of his sense of humor and even a bit of the playfulness that she liked about him.

He might complain about his aching and aging bones and graying hair, but sometimes he behaved like a much younger man. And his skills in bedplay revealed no waning of desire or vigor, as was the case with some of the men she saw.

His body remained fit and strong, and he could outfight and outlast most of the warriors here in Dunnedin. She smiled again at the thought of Rob's insults. She wanted to watch this battle. The sound of footsteps approaching down the corridor made her wrap a blanket around herself. A soft knock preceded the door's opening.

"Robena?" The Lady Anice stood in the doorway holding a bundle of clothes. Hers?

"My lady," she said, curtsying as best she could. "I beg yer pardon for being here." Though she was welcome in the keep, Robena tried to stay out of view of the lady and the chieftain, Struan. Why bring trouble down on her head by flaunting her presence?

"Here," the lady said as she tried to hand the bundle to her.

Easing an arm out from within the blanket, Robena reached for them, but the lady laughed and walked to the bed instead. She placed them there and walked back to the door.

"My thanks for bringing these. I wasna certain how I was to leave without them."

"Iain asked to have them washed last night. He rarely asks for anything, so the servants hurried to do this for him." The lady lifted the latch and dropped it, facing her.

"Ye ken that ye are welcome to stay here with him, Robena."

"Lady Anice," Robena began, unsure of how to say what she wanted to without sounding ungrateful or unappreciative. "I ken my place, my lady. I cannot thank ye enough for making a place for me at table and making it known to all that I am welcome." Robena paused then and nodded, knowing that her next words would come close to an admission she probably should not make.

"'Twould be too easy to get the wrong idea if I stayed here with him."

Something was dangerously different between them already and staying here would just confuse her—them—even more. The contentment she had in her life came from knowing who and what she was, and her place here in the MacKendimen Clan. To blur the lines and pretend to be something, someone, that she was not and could never be, would leave her wanting when he left. Nay, that was not the truth. She *would* miss Iain when he returned to Dunbarton, but it would be so much worse if she allowed herself to want more than she could have. If she wanted him.

She swallowed against the sudden tightness in her throat and smiled at Anice, trying to express a confidence in her words and acceptance that she didn't truly feel right now. The lady, a few years younger than Robena was, studied her then and tilted her hair as though considering something about her.

"I wonder—who would get the wrong idea if you remained here with him?" she asked.

When Robena would have answered back, to point out the problems that could arise if she acted as though she mattered as other than the village harlot, Anice smiled and shook her head.

"Worry not, Robena," the lady said. "Ye have never overstepped yerself here in all the years I have kenned ye. I would not expect ye to do otherwise." She lifted the latch once more and tugged the door open. Robena could see the lady's maid waiting for her in the corridor.

"Though it might be something to see if ye decided 'twas time to overstep the boundaries ye have placed around yer life, and to claim a different place for yerself."

So many possible replies rolled in her thoughts, and yet none would come to her tongue, leaving Robena silent and speechless as the lady left. Unable to face the challenge leveled at her in those words, Robena dropped the blanket and dressed. 'Twould be a poor show of gratitude if she did not get to the yard and watch Iain fight there. After all he'd done for her, and after he'd generously overlooked her lack of attention this last day and night.

Once garbed, she wove a braid to keep her hair from being blown wild in the November winds and put her cloak around her shoulders. Her stomach growled as she walked through the hall, reminding her of the meal she'd left untouched abovestairs, yet she did not stop. Not here. She could break her fast in her cottage later.

She'd made it almost to the door when the laird stepped out in front of her.

Struan MacKendimen ruled the clan, though Rob carried out many duties that the older man should. Five years ago, Rob's arrival back at Struan's call had revealed the secret of their relationship, and the balance of everything had shifted within the clan. As the elder of Struan's sons, though his natural son rather than his legitimate one, Rob had turned out to be the better one to lead the clan.

But that was only known after Alesander MacKendimen, the other son, had married the Lady

Anice MacNab and was killed in a strange incident on his way home to Dunnedin for the birth of their bairn.

Robena would have spit on the ground at the thought of the dead man had she not been inside the keep, and had it not been Struan before her.

"What do ye here, Robena?" he asked, looking her over and not bothering to keep that slight look of disgust hidden.

"I am on my way home, laird," she said, curtsying slightly as she tried to hurry away. In some ways, Struan had the same hardness in him that his younger son had. Once more, she stopped herself from spitting at the memory of Alesander MacKendimen.

"Do ye have some task for me?" she asked. Even though it was a lie, she invoked the name of one of the few women the laird did respect, and she hoped it would protect her. "I will be going to Moira's on the way, if ye need me to take a message there?"

The laird crossed his arms over his chest and seemed to think on her words before he shook his head. Then he nodded at the door.

"I ken that Anice has said otherwise, but I dinna want ye in my hall," he said. "So, get ye gone from my keep." He raised his hand as though to slap her but dropped it with a grunt at her instead.

Sometimes a person, a man, would strike out rather than waiting to be struck himself. Robena thought this was Struan's way now, for everyone here knew of his own son's cruelty, and that Robena had been one of his victims—if a whore could be considered as such.

Watching him now, she thought that their encounters only served to remind Struan of the terrible sins his now-deceased son had committed, which he had failed to stop. Something not many men would wish to remember or dwell upon.

She did not say a word more, for he was laird, and no one, especially not the village whore, could naysay him and escape unpunished. Even Rob's intercession would not save her if Struan was intent on doing something. So, she did what a good whore would do—she bowed her head and made herself as small and unthreatening as possible as she walked the few paces left between her and the doors.

The winds caught her as she ran, past the stables, past the yard and out through the gate, toward the village. She did not stop until she reached her cottage and slammed the door closed. Leaning against it, she could not keep the tears from flowing.

The Lady Anice's words about challenging the boundaries of her life had shaken Robena in a way that surprised her. With no chance at children of her own, she had begun helping other women to birth theirs. The knowledge that Alesander's attack had taken that possibility from her bothered her more and more with each passing year. At least her own mother had had Robena—for company, for help, for something to pass on after her death. Robena could have nothing, no one, like that.

She'd fought off the growing despair as the years passed, but it was getting harder to do it. She found joy, or rather enjoyment, where and with whom she could, and tried to ignore the deep sense of emptiness at the core of her soul. The thing that frightened her most was not that she'd lost her purpose, but that she was losing her hope for a life fulfilled.

He never saw the blow coming.

One moment Iain was dodging Rob's punches and deflecting the strikes of Rob's staff without much effort at all, and the next, Iain was eating the dirt of the yard. Loud laughter and raucous insults rang out across the yard at his defeat. His boasting that had preceded their bout did not help him now as he stood and brushed the dirt off his face and spat it from his mouth.

"What happened, old man?" Rob asked, smacking Iain on his back. "Ye said ye would triumph this time." The knowing look in his eyes told Iain that his friend knew exactly what had happened. And, damn him, Rob would be right.

Just as he had positioned himself for that final attack, Iain had seen Robena come running out of the keep like Satan himself was chasing her. Head down, she did not look up or about as she ran past them and everyone else who had tasks or duties inside the walls. He'd turned his gaze to follow her path, and Rob had struck him down. He did not care that he lost, for it had happened before and would again, but he did care that something had happened to her within.

"What do you think happened?" he asked Rob. His friend did not deny witnessing her flight from the hall.

"Anice was headed to yer chamber with her clothing when I left her," Rob explained.

That could not be the reason, for Anice had accepted Robena's place in the clan and allowed her entrance into the hall when she wished. He shrugged.

"I dinna ken. But I do not like the way she ran away."

"Ye can find out the reason later," Rob said. "I'm guessing she willna join us for supper."

"Though she is willing to do anything I ask of her"—he paused at Rob's raised brow—"*that* is the one thing she will not do." Iain let out his breath and shook his head.

"She keeps to herself, Iain. Well, she keeps to her own matters, and helps out the midwife when needed. Anice has gotten her to take meals in the hall only three times that I can remember. I rarely speak to her because she fears someone might think the wrong thing." Rob had grown up with her. Run wild as children with her. Loved her …

"And she wants for nothing?" he asked. How could a woman be part of a clan, part of a village, and yet not be?

When Rob did not answer him, Iain glanced over to find his friend staring at him, his gaze narrow and direct.

"Why does this concern ye? She is here for yer comfort on yer visits. Why does the rest of her life matter to ye, as long as ye are not inconvenienced when ye are paying yer coin for her time?"

Iain could not explain his reaction then. Without

warning he swung at Rob and knocked him back on his heels. Not giving him a chance to rebound, Iain swung again and again until Rob finally fought back. The sounds of the crowd gathering and shouting faded as he threw himself into this battle. This time he gave as good as he got against his younger opponent, and when he tackled Rob and held him down, the rage or confusion cleared and he saw the smirk on his friend's face.

He pulled back his arm to deliver the final blow and realized that this had been the purpose of Rob's words— to make him understand the truth of the matter.

It did matter. It did concern him. She concerned him.

"God damn ye to hell, Rob," he said as he pushed himself off Rob and stood, brushing the dirt from his hands. "Ye ken."

"She matters to ye, does she not?" Rob asked quietly, blowing hard from the exertion of the fight. He wiped the back of his hand across his mouth and spit. "Do ye wonder why?"

"Do not push this, Rob." Iain turned away then, unwilling to show his uncertainty to his friend.

They turned as someone called out. Brodie, Rob's other childhood friend and now one of his most loyal warriors, walked towards them. Iain thought to escape, but the man's information kept him there. Something had happened at the mill that needed Rob's attention. As Rob called out orders, Iain decided to join them.

Physical labor had helped him sort through his dilemmas in the past, so he added his name to the group being sent to see to the matter. Within an hour, they were mounted and riding out of the keep towards the west.

And, in spite of Rob's sly smile when Iain asked, he arranged to send a message to Robena about his absence.

Aye, she matters, he thought as he rode with the others towards the mill.

Chapter 5

Iain had forgotten how damned and bitterly cold the Highlands could be when winter moved in to stay. They'd reached the mill some miles from the keep to discover that an attack had left the miller and his son injured, sent his family into hiding and the mill itself damaged. Now, three days later, they were riding back to Dunnedin Keep after leaving guards in place and packing up the miller and his family to return with them. He let his thoughts drift to a warm place to sleep, a hot bath, and a cooked meal—simple things—things he'd missed these last days and nights.

More so, he'd missed Robena.

He told himself it was because he'd planned to spend these weeks with her. And that he knew she was waiting for him. None of those previous plans mattered now, for over the last few days he'd finally decided that he wanted her, and not as his whore. Not even as his leman.

As his…wife.

Oh, he was not ignoring the challenges to getting what—who—he wanted, for Iain did not delude himself into thinking this would be an easy matter to resolve.

Many people would have their say, whether invited to or not, and many of his kith and kin would object and place obstacles in his path. Hell, if he was thinking straight, he would ken better than to take another step into the quagmire this would undoubtedly become.

As they rode through the village, Iain kept watch for her along the paths. She could be in any number of places, not expecting his return this day. When they'd arrived at the mill and inspected the damage, Rob had, at his request and with a great amount of smirking, sent word to her that Iain had accompanied him with the message that called for Pol, the blacksmith. Their path did not take them near to her cottage, so Iain would have to wait.

The lady stood waiting at the top of the steps leading into the keep, and servants took their horses and offered them cups of mulled wine. Anice ran this household better than even the most experienced commander of warriors did his men. He knew that she would have already made arrangements for everything they needed on their return.

"Food waits in yer chambers, to hold ye until supper," she announced to the group. "And a hot bath." Rob leaned in when he reached her, and Iain could tell what he'd asked from the blush that rose in her cheeks that had nothing to do with the cold winds swirling around them.

"I have tasks to see to, Rob. Ye can wash yerself." She pushed Rob away with a playful slap on his arm and nodded her greeting to Iain. When he reached her, she touched his arm.

"A bath awaits ye, Iain," she said.

"My thanks, Anice. My old bones would like nothing more than a long soak in a steaming tub." He knew the lie in his words and what he'd omitted, and her gaze narrowed as he met it. She knew as well.

"Iain, I sent word to Robena, but she has not come."

Knowing when Rob had sent word ahead to his wife, Iain understood that there had been plenty of time for word to reach Robena as well. Not attending him in his chambers was not due to a lack of notice. Was it something else, then? Mayhap she tended to another birthing.

Or was needed in some other matter?

Disappointed, Iain drank his wine, soaked in his bath until the water grew cold, and was dressed in time for supper. When he entered the hall and went to the table, he found his place had been moved, from next to Rob over to Struan's other side, next to a woman he did not recognize. With a slight bow to the laird, he sat.

"This is my late wife's sister, Gunna," Struan said as Iain settled there. "She is visiting with us, but I dinna think ye have met before?"

"Nay, Struan, I think we have," Iain said, in what he hoped was a pleasant voice. "Lady." He nodded at the woman, who looked to be close to his own age.

"I met ye when I met yer brother," the woman said. "'Twas some years ago, and I was sorry to hear of his passing."

He remembered little about this woman but did recollect that she was one of the four women under consideration to marry his brother a score and ten years ago. Though initially attracted to several of those brought for his inspection, Duncan had fallen in love with his Margaret at first glance and remained that way until his death.

"My thanks. He is missed even now," Iain offered.

Duncan was missed by all of his kith and kin, and his widow had not yet recovered from her grief. Iain doubted Margaret would. When he looked at Struan, Iain saw grief in the laird's eyes as well, for Struan and Duncan had been fostered together and had remained friends until Duncan's passing. The laird had even sent his natural son to Duncan when he thought it necessary. A glance over at Rob told him that Rob had heard the words. "So, what brings ye to Dunnedin, lady?" he asked politely as he tried to push their talk back to a less painful topic.

"Struan invited me to visit. 'Tis been a while since I was here."

Anice's choking cough drew attention. Rob patted his wife's back and offered her the cup there to ease it. Turning back to Gunna and Struan, he nodded, all the while wondering over Anice's reaction to the woman's words. Iain had sat at the tables of nobles all over Scotland, and understood how to conduct a polite and meaningless conversation.

Rob spoke about the matter of the attack on the mill and miller, which seemed to be more about a rogue band of thieves than another clan's incursion onto

MacKendimen lands. As winter set in, these outlaws grew bold in seeking supplies to see them through the dark and cold months of December and January. Come spring, they would be back on the roads and in the forests, where Rob and his men could flush them out.

The meal, filling and hot, was served, and the time passed as he exchanged words with Struan's kin. A few strange glances from Rob, after Anice's coughing, made him uneasy, and he would have to find out what Rob meant. When Anice stood, Gunna did as well, and they left the table together. From the way that Anice walked off without her once they reached the bottom of the steps, Iain understood there were no warm feelings between the two. Which made Gunna's acceptance of Struan's invitation even more curious.

"She is a fine woman, would ye not say, Iain?" Struan asked. The laird held up his cup and Iain watched as it was filled by a waiting servant. He tried to put just the right reply together before speaking.

"She seems to be, Struan. I have not seen her since her family was negotiating for her to marry Duncan all those years ago."

"Gunna was widowed years ago and is open to remarrying." Well, the man could be direct when he wanted to be. Now it was Rob's turn to choke. Struan glared at his son and turned back to Iain. "I am sure yer family is urging ye to remarry. The commander of the MacKillop's warriors is in fine mettle to marry and have children."

"As I have told my nephew, if I choose to marry again, I will be certain to let everyone ken of my decision to do so." He tried to speak the words in an even tone, but his anger at Struan's presumption grew.

"If ye had a wife in yer bed, ye wouldna have to chase after that whore like a dog in heat." Struan whispered his opinion through clenched teeth, but still loud enough for Iain to hear. Loud enough for Rob as well.

Iain had stood, grabbed hold of Struan, and pulled him to his feet before he even realized it. The utter silence surrounding them brought him to his senses as he realized that everyone there was watching. He was moments and inches away from offering a grievous insult to the laird of the MacKendimens, one his nephew would have to deal with. One that could break years of friendships *and alliances.*

The words about Struan's own actions, chasing a woman like a dog in heat until she cuckolded her own husband and bore Rob, were not words to be spoken aloud. They would not surprise anyone here, for the story of Rob's beginnings was familiar, but to remind the laird of his failures and to call Rob's mother an adulteress before this clan would do no one any good at all. And, worse, 'twould do much harm.

"Just so," Iain said as he released his hold of the older man. He stepped back and offered a slight bow before turning and walking down the steps and out of the hall.

Rob caught up with him before he'd made it back to his chamber and followed him within.

"I thank ye for not blurting out anything about the circumstances of my birth," his friend said. "Though I could see ye wanted to say it to his face."

"Secrets revealed are still never easy to hear."

"I didna ken why he brought Gunna here, for 'tis been years since her last visit here."

"There was some problem between her and Anice, then?" Iain could decipher it in Anice's face, and in the way she'd left her aunt-by-marriage behind.

"Aye. Gunna was here when Anice was young and inexperienced in dealing with her life and challenges. Gunna reminds her of bad decisions and behaviors, long after Anice grew into the woman she is now."

"That might be the reason behind Struan's words then. Regret? Embarrassment over how he lived his own life and the choices he's made?"

Rob crossed his arms over his chest, letting out his breath as he nodded. Iain began gathering up his clothing out of the trunk in the corner and stuffing it in a leather sack.

"If ye wanted to be charitable, ye could think of it as advice he's giving to ye, so ye would not make mistakes as he has." Iain shook his head, partly to deny that possibility, and partly in disbelief that Rob would defend the man. "What are ye doing?"

"I think a few days in the village might do me some good," Iain said. "Send word if ye have need of me. Ye ken where I will be."

"So, ye have no plans to marry again?" Rob asked.

"Nay." Iain shoved another shirt in the bag. "Aye." He tossed everything on the bed and put his hands on his hips. "I would love to have what ye have, Rob. I miss Elisabeth and I miss what a man can have with a woman he loves."

"Are ye seeking to marry, then?" Rob goaded him. Iain let out an exasperated groan.

"Jamie wants me to remarry and have bairns, to ally another clan with ours. Struan thinks marrying again is a good plan—for me but not himself, clearly. Ye, too?"

"Bairns?"

"I have only two score and five years on me, Rob. I can still make bairns." If he had not glanced up at that exact moment, he would have missed the alarm that crossed Rob's face. It was gone so quickly Iain wondered if he'd even seen it there.

"Right now, I want to go and spend some time with a woman I ken who will not ask me questions."

Iain tugged the sack closed and picked it up. "I think I will stay there until Gunna has gone." Rob's laugh taunted him then, but he resisted the urge to say more or to punch his friend. He opened the door and motioned for him to leave. "Give my regards to Anice, if ye will."

"About Anice and bairns," Rob began. "She is carrying."

A broad and proud smile filled his face at the announcement. Iain smacked Rob's shoulder at this news, for it had been almost five years since Anice had given birth to her son Craig with no sign of bearing another.

This explained Rob's strange reaction to the question of bairns earlier.

"Ye have my best wishes, Rob. 'Tis not kenned yet?"

"Nay, she wishes to wait a bit longer before announcing it. Moira kens, as do a few others."

"I will not speak of it until ye give me leave." With that, he pulled the door behind him, forcing Rob to move along.

"Iain, why do I get the feeling that ye are running away?"

Iain answered with a crude gesture and walked away, unwilling to say more.

In a way, he supposed he *was* escaping. Escaping from Struan's plan to make a match between Iain and Struan's cousin. Escaping from the need to pretend he did not want to be with Robena. As he made his way to the stable to ready his own horse, Iain decided that he was escaping, but instead of running away, he was running *to*... her.

As he rode like the flames of hell were pursuing him, he realized that he had made a decision to marry. Not to a woman most would expect or want him to marry. When he arrived at her cottage and stood before her door, he understood that his biggest challenge, the one he might not overcome, was the woman waiting within for him.

Iain knocked softly and waited for permission to enter.

When it did not come, he lifted the latch and opened the door slowly. Careful not to allow too much of the cold in, he quickly closed and secured it against the growing force of the winds. Waiting for his eyes to adjust to the low light, he finally found her. Not lying on the pallet, but sitting in the one large chair, sound asleep.

He walked softly over to her and crouched before the chair. Her breathing was deep and even as she slept, unaware of his arrival. Then he noticed that her hair tumbled loosely over her, and that she wore only the blanket wrapped around her. Her bare feet peeked out at the bottom and rested on the floor. If the fire had been stronger when it was laid, 'twas not now, and she shivered in her sleep.

Iain put the bag down and found some wood to add to the fire. It grew stronger and threw more heat as the new logs caught, and he watched as her shivering eased. Returning to the place before her, he sat, and with a care not to wake her, lifted her feet up and put them on his lap.

Then, after rubbing his hands together briskly to warm them up, he laid them on her feet and stroked up under the blanket in a very slow path. His hands could almost encircle her ankles, so he did, sliding down and up, along the front of her shins and on the back of her legs. Her loud sigh was the only warning before she woke.

Robena opened her eyes then, though she wanted to sit here and enjoy the feel and the heat of his touch on her feet and legs. She hadn't realized how chilly it had gotten, because she'd sat down and had promptly fallen asleep.

So much for her intention to wait and be ready for his *return. H*e sat at her feet, or rather under her feet, stroking her, bringing the warmth of his strong hands to her chilled skin. Leaning forward, she smiled at him when he looked up at her.

"I wanted to be ready for ye," she said.

"Ye did not come to the keep when Anice sent word."

If she did not have a care, she would hear the disappointment in his voice and allow it to soften her resolve about him. She lifted her feet from his lap then and he allowed it. Reaching down, she took his hands in hers.

"I couldna."

She tugged until he stood and let the blanket around her drop as she reached out to caress his legs. Beginning at his knees, she stroked up much as he had, but onto his thighs, feeling the well-defined muscles there. His breathing changed as she slid onto her knees before him.

"Couldna or wouldna?" he asked in a breathy whisper.

Did he think her willful? That she would ignore his call for no reason but her own? Robena sat back on her heels and tilted her head up to meet his gaze. The erection brought on by her caresses was visible there in the way the woolen plaid tented out from his groin.

"The laird forbade me from entering the keep."

She felt his strength as he pulled her to her feet and admitted to herself that she loved it. The way he could move her at his will. He could hold her up while he entered her, while he took her standing or against the wall. He could stretch out his arms over her body and hold her immobile as he tormented her with his mouth and his cock. Never once had he used that strength in a way she did not wish.

"But Anice has welcomed ye there," he said.

"Anice is the lady of the keep, but Struan is still laird,

Iain. He has every right to bar me from entering, or to punish me if I disobey his word. Ye ken that, ye do." She moved back a step and let the blanket fall completely away. "So, I'm afraid ye will have to visit me here if ye want me."

She found herself waiting for him to say he would come here. That he did want her. But the icy expression that covered his eyes worried her.

"Iain? Is aught wrong?"

"Nay, Robena. Not with ye. But 'twould seem that Struan is up to some game."

He reached for her then and slid his hands up and down on her arms gently. When he looked at her, his eyes were warm and alive. "I do not mind visiting ye here at all. As ye can see, I had planned to do that already." He canted his head towards the pallet, and she noticed the leather bag there.

"Will ye tell me what he did?" she asked.

The laird had been openly hostile to her, but he could not do that to Iain. Not with the long history of friendship between their families. Not with the position of respect each held in their clans. Struan had changed with his son's death and with Rob's marriage to Anice. He'd broken his word and few trusted him, but fewer still raised a voice to question his authority. Rob had made it clear that he was serving as tanist until a new chieftain was needed.

"He brought his late wife's cousin here to visit."

That did not seem so strange, or even a bad thing to Robena. With a clan as large as the MacKendimens, kin came from all over their lands to visit, stay, foster, or live.

She shrugged, not seeing the problem.

"For me to consider marrying."

Chapter 6

That dark and angry expression was back in his eyes, and his face was like carved stone. He was a man clearly opposed to marrying again. In a way, it made her feel more at ease. She was certain when she'd seen that wanting look in his eyes on his first night here that it had meant something dangerous. Now, with his anger at Struan for trying to arrange a marriage for him, she understood that he was not being foolish in feeling more for her than he should.

More than either could allow.

"I can understand why he would do such a thing, Iain. Ye are a man yet in yer prime. Ye are connected by blood and oath to the chieftain of the powerful MacKillop Clan. Ye have much to offer a woman and her family looking to make an advantageous alliance."

"So I have been told," he said.

Robena walked past him and poured them both some ale. Handing him one of the cups, she realized he wished to talk more than he wished to tup. She smiled at that, for most men did not spend their precious coin to sit and talk with a whore. She found she liked these times as much as she did the other things they did together.

"My thanks," he said, holding the cup up and nodding to her. He drank deeply as she realized that was another thing she liked in him—his willingness to acknowledge service and servants. Watching as he took another mouthful, she could not remember a time when Struan had offered thanks to anyone who did his bidding. Other than to Anice.

The fire would begin to ebb soon, so she grabbed up the blanket, tossed it over the others already on the pallet, and climbed under the warm layers. As she slid towards the wall and placed pillows behind her back, she held up the covers for Iain.

They'd spent many hours just like this—sitting on the pallet, discussing this or that, coupling when the urge came over one or the other or both of them. He finished the last of the ale and tugged on his belt. With the fire behind him, his shape outlined by the flickering flames, she watched as his body was exposed.

She'd seen worse and she'd had a few better, but none affected her as his did. As he pulled his shirt over his head, she remembered the feel of the muscles in his thighs and knew how hard the muscles in his arse would feel as he thrust into her. She liked to cup them with her palms. He turned to put his garments aside and the whole length of his prick could be seen against the fire's light. She would need both hands to wrap around that.

"Are ye hungry, lass?" he asked as he watched her

face. Walking towards her, he offered, "Do ye need something to eat?"

Robena could not help herself for she laughed aloud at his words. He'd meant them kindly, truly he had, never considering their other meaning. But then Iain had never been a coarse man when it came to fleshly desires and needs. He frowned for a moment, and then understanding struck and he joined her in laughing. He knelt on the pallet and climbed next to her, his cock creating a tent of the covers when she tugged the woolen blankets over the both of them.

"So, you do not wish to marry again?" she asked as he settled next to her. Iain moved in close, sliding his arm behind her and shifting her so they touched. His warmth flowed off him, adding to her comfort. She hadn't known how cold she'd become until he was next to her.

"I have sworn for the last five years that I did not wish to," he admitted. He reached around her to clasp her hand in his, entwining their fingers.

"Are ye changing yer thinking on it, then?"

Before he answered her, he reached his other hand down and rested it on her belly. Even through the blankets, she could feel the heat of his touch. His long fingers splayed out, some over her belly and some nearer to the curls between her legs. Though he did nothing more, she found it difficult to breathe.

"If I found the right woman, aye, I would think on it," he said, his words now spoken close to her ear.

He shifted, and his cock pressed against her hip under the bedcovers. Now he began to swirl his fingers lightly over the covers, but she felt every movement as though he touched her flesh to flesh.

"Not Struan's cousin?" she managed to ask in halting, affected words.

"Nay! Not Gunna," he said. "If I marry again, 'twill not be that woman."

"Good." The word escaped her lips.

"Good? Ye dinna wish me to marry, then?" he asked, his voice teasing her as much as his relentless, gentle caresses did.

He made no pretense about his motives, for he pushed the covers down and caressed her breasts. The rough skin on his thumbs made her ache as he rubbed her nipples.

When he leaned down and took the tight point of flesh into his mouth, she lost the ability to think. His teeth clasped it and he licked it with his tongue while his lips sucked hard. The moan that echoed into the cottage could not be helped or held in. She grabbed his head with her free hand, holding him there. When he lifted his gaze to hers, the wickedness in his blue gaze foretold of the pleasures ahead.

"So, I shouldna marry again?" he asked as he lowered his face once more to torment the other nipple. He slid his hand down now, down and down until he spread his fingers over her curls. Her legs fell open at his caress.

His every touch sent her wits scattering, and her ability to think just disappeared. "Lass? Ye dinna wish me to marry?"

"If ye marry, we willna do this," she finally said. "Any of this."

She pulled free of him, pushed him on his back, climbed over him, and slid onto his length. He reached up and guided her hips down, hissing at the sheer pleasure of the friction inside her. Then she rode him, easing up and down, faster and faster. He filled her and it felt good to her.

"Ye would refuse me?" he asked as his breathing quickened.

She lost her concentration for a moment at that question, and he took advantage of it. Taking hold of her waist, he pushed up and rolled over, thrusting in deeply when her back hit the pallet. He was tall enough that he could rest his elbows next to her shoulders when they were like this. He smoothed her hair out of her face and stared at her. As she shifted her hips to allow his prick in deeper, she gave him her honest answer.

"Ye are a faithful man, Iain," she whispered. "Ye would not share the bed of any other woman, noble or whore, if ye were married."

He kissed her then, not moving anything but his mouth on hers. He did not close his eyes then but stared at hers with a puzzled expression. Had he not realized it? Surely, he must have, for his behavior was different than most noblemen. 'Twas one of the many things she lov…liked about him.

"'Tis a good thing I am not married, then."

Iain watched as her eyes changed from green and bright to something dark. He eased out of her and pushed back in, listening to her breathing as he did. She closed her eyes, leaned her head back and shifted her knees up to his hips. His next thrust filled her and she gasped at it. He let go of his control and his hunger for her took over. When she moved against him, he quickened his pace and rocked in as far as he could on every thrust.

Her breathy sighs became moans and then soft screams as her inner core tightened around his flesh and he felt his seed begin to release.

He wanted this woman as he'd wanted no other before. He admitted that, as the need to have her and possess her took over in those last few moments of satisfaction. Iain leaned down and suckled her neck, pulling the tender skin between his teeth as she screamed out her own release. He'd marked her.

"Iain," she whispered as she caressed his head, running her fingers through his hair as her breathing eased to a slower pace. "That was…" She paused, and her fingers slipped down onto his back. "Simply wonderful." He felt her body relax then. "I thank ye for that."

"What do ye mean?" he asked, easing out of her body and gathering her close.

"For again seeing to my needs," she explained.

"A man should see to a woman's pleasure, Robena."

"Ah, but a man does not worry over a whore's pleasure or pain," she whispered. "'Tis only about getting his coin's worth, in whatever way he wants it." Iain lifted her face so she had to meet his eyes then. Were all the men she…saw…like that with her? Oblivious to her needs or desire? Seeing the honesty in her gaze, he understood the truth of her life in that moment. He wanted to punch the wall.

"Do ye never wish to stop this, Robena? To be something, someone, other than a who—who ye are?" She did not reply for a few long moments. "Did ye never want to marry and have bairns of yer own instead of helping other women have theirs?"

"I always thought I would, Iain. That I would find a man who would accept me." She let out a sigh then, and closed her eyes. He should have taken it as a warning for her next words. "Since I canna have bairns, there are not many men who would want me as their wife."

She spoke the words without feeling, and yet he felt like he'd been struck by lightning. Robena changed before his eyes, pulling back from him and moving away, becoming a stranger right before him. She stood then and walked over and sat in the chair. That she paused to grab up and put on her shift told him more about the true distance between them than he suspected she understood.

Iain pushed himself up to sit and watched her. Robena may have spoken the words as though they mattered not, as though she'd accepted the terrible declaration, but her reaction told him how much she felt the pain of it. He struggled as he confronted both his need to find one of those men to thrash, and his guilt for never having considered her true situation. Searching for the right words to say, she surprised him by finding them herself.

"I faced the truth of it many years ago, Iain. I just choose not to think on it much, or to speak of it," she explained as she stared at the flames in the hearth instead of him. "In a way, it makes my life easier, considering..."

She moved only her hand in a graceful turn to indicate her world, reminding him that he was in the cottage of the village harlot. If he were honest with himself, it bothered him. Selfishly, he knew, for it upset his own plans and needs, too.

He did want to marry again—he wanted to marry her, to keep her for himself, and he did want bairns. It took but one glance at the misery she lived with and tried to put aside for Iain to want to scream out at the unfairness of this. For her.

For her.

"Come," he said softly. He straightened out the jumble of bedcovers and readied them for her return. "Ye will catch a chill sitting there."

She stood but remained there staring at the fire for several minutes before coming back to the pallet. He thought she might try to hold herself away from him, so he was pleased when she settled in his arms. He let a short while pass, during which neither of them slept, before broaching the topic again.

"Yer pardon, lass," he whispered against her hair. "I had no right to bring that up." He kissed her head. "My nephew says I can be worse than his own mother when it comes to meddling in matters not of my concern."

The kiss on his chest was her reply. He would leave it at that for now and try to sort out how he felt about this new twist. As the hours passed and her breathing fell into a slow, even pace, Iain lay there holding her close, unable to let her revelation go. A memory of the strange expression on Rob's face at Iain's mention of having bairns made him understand that others here knew about this.

When the sun rose and any doubts over his original intention were settled for him, Iain eased from Robena's arms, having a care not to wake her, and made his way back to the keep. Rob could give him the answers and advice he needed. To ask Robena would simply cause her more pain.

And as a warrior, a man experienced in battle and strategy, Iain knew he needed to know as much as possible about his opponents, their strengths and their weaknesses. In this matter of marriage, he knew that this battle would be no less formidable than one played out on a field of war. Iain planned to win this, just as he had won others. When he found Rob in the stables, his friend's grim expression told him that he'd been expected.

"Ye kenned?"

At Rob's nod, he motioned for Iain to follow away from where men were carrying out their chores, and Iain followed. They walked out to the yard and stopped at the fence. No one was training there yet, so they could speak without being overheard.

"What did she tell ye?" Rob asked, leaning his arms on the top rail of the fence, not meeting Iain's gaze.

"That she canna have bairns." He shrugged. "There's not much more to say after that."

His friend stood in silence, not adding a word, until it struck Iain. There was so much more to this. Staring at the back of Rob's head, Iain finally understood the question that had nagged at him about Robena's situation in this village. The truth at the heart of how she survived as the harlot of Dunnedin.

"Ye are her protector." Though spoken quietly, the accusation and the words and the possible truth within them made him want to howl out in anger and frustration. And jealousy. Did he still fuck her? Had Iain misread the relationship between them? Rob spun around and faced him, his answer there for Iain to read on his face.

"I am faithful to my wife, Iain. I have ever been, and will always be," Rob ground out the words. "Ye dinna understand."

In one single moment, all the incongruities formed a pattern in his mind. The way things were here. The way Robena was treated—by the villagers, by the men, by even the laird. Not like any village harlot Iain had ever known. Too many choices. Too much control. No whore had that much, unless there was a strong and powerful man who gave it to her.

"Ye are her protector," he repeated, waiting for Rob to deny his part in this, all the while knowing he could not.

"Aye. Protector, but not lover." Rob let out a breath at the admission. It still did not explain everything, but …

"Anice and I are both her protectors."

Iain knew there had been some great service provided by Robena to the Lady Anice when Rob had returned here from Dunbarton, which would explain her part in this. He stared at Rob, waiting for the rest to follow.

"Anice does it out of gratitude," he said. "Robena

offered her advice and good counsel when Anice first married me. 'Twas a time when she needed help that none but Robena could give."

Iain had heard the rumors, or stories, even over in his village at the time when Anice had married Rob's half-brother and ended up beaten and nearly dead on her wedding night. A wedding night such as that would have put any woman off the marriage bed, and yet Iain knew Anice and Rob were happy and content in their marriage now. Iain could imagine what kind of advice the lady had needed from the harlot, Rob's former lover.

"And ye?" Iain asked. "Do ye stand in friendship to her?"

Iain could not ignore that the two had been friends for a long time. Rare for a man and woman. And though he'd like to overlook it, the fact was, Rob had shared her bed before he'd married Anice. Whatever words he'd been expecting, he did not expect the next ones.

"I protect her because 'tis my fault that she nearly died and that she willna ever bear children." Rob's face paled and his eyes grew bleak and empty. Or so Iain thought until he got a better look. Nay, they were filled with loathing and sorrow.

"Yer fault? How, Rob?" Surely his friend would never harm Robena, so what could have happened?

"On his—their—wedding night, Sandy sent his men to Robena, after allowing them to watch as he beat and…had…Anice. He suspected that Anice had betrayed him with another, and he punished her, nearly killing her that night." Iain's gut roiled at the story he was hearing now. "Then, Sandy turned them loose like a pack of wolves and sent them to slake their lust and needs on the whore he kenned was my friend." Rob grimaced as he spoke and clenched his fists.

"He paid them, paid his men, to *see to her.*" Rob spit in the dirt then, and Iain's stomach heaved at the thought of what those men had done. "Because she was my friend, Iain."

Iain had been in battle and had seen the aftermath of brutality that could follow the euphoria or disappointment. But men full of drink, paid to do such a thing, defied everything he knew. And all because Rob's half-brother was jealous of anything Rob had or did. Iain had seen it before Rob had been sent to Dunbarton to live and train with Iain's brother Duncan. But now, he had to face the knowledge that two women —one whom he respected and one whom he loved—suffered because of the uncontrolled madness and jealousy of one man, and it sickened him.

Rob turned, leaned his back against the fence, and crossed his arms over his chest. As Iain stared off at the keep for a few moments before saying anything more, he struggled to resist the urge to retch.

"So, I have made certain that she chooses what will happen in her life. She doesna have to whore, but she has the freedom now to choose whom she fucks and who she doesna. The men here, the people, ken that I will see to any trouble that comes her way."

Iain was proud of the young man who stood here now and knew his brother would have been as well if Duncan had lived to see this.

"And if she wanted to leave here?" Iain asked.

"She can." Rob turned to face him. "Do ye think to take her back with ye to Dunbarton?"

"Aye."

One quiet word and his life had changed the moment he spoke it aloud to another. Now, 'twas not conjecture or private. Now, 'twas a possibility.

"And what has Robena said about it? Does she wish to leave?" It was Iain's turn to remain silent. "Ye have not asked her, have ye?"

"Nay."

"Ye have been here for days, Iain. When do ye think to tell her that ye want her to go back to Dunbarton?"

He'd had a plan in mind when he arrived—he would allow them to settle into the comfortable pattern they liked from previous visits first, and then he would ask her.

But his time here was closer to its beginning than its end, so he thought there was plenty of time.

"I was going to ask her soon. Do ye think she will?" he asked. If anyone knew Robena, it was Rob.

"Anice might ken Robena's mind on this, or mayhap Moira would. How will Jamie react to ye bringing a leman back with ye? Will that not put a pause in his plans to marry ye off? I would think that most prospective brides are put off by the presence of a man's mistress."

Iain realized the mistake immediately. Rob did not understand that Iain would be proposing marriage to Robena, not asking her to be his mistress.

"I want her to wife, Rob."

If Rob's face cracked and crumbled into dust, Iain would not be surprised. His expression took on the look of stone—cold and empty—as he stared at Iain as though he had not understood the words.

"Are ye daft, man?" Rob finally asked. "Have ye no idea of what lies ahead if ye try to take her to wife? Ye command The MacKillop's men. Ye live in his keep. A woman who has lived as a whore will not be welcomed there."

"I have thought of little else, Rob." He spat out the words. "I have given my life and my service, first to my brother and then to his son. I have expected little or nothing in return but a place with my kin. I ken they cannot accept her openly. I ken she will not have an easy time of it. But I want her. I want her as my wife." He'd almost not recognized the anger and the desire within him, and how much he'd decided his course, until he told Rob.

"And now? Does the knowledge that she cannot give ye bairns change yer thinking on it?"

Her admission had given him pause, but they did not change wanting her. Or wanting to marry her. Rob's explanation made his blood boil at the pain she must have suffered before learning of the loss of her ability to have bairns. Yet, from her own words and those of the villagers, she was nothing but kind to everyone. She still helped whoever needed her, she assisted women through their own travails of childbirth, and she still saw to the needs of the men she took to her bed.

"I admit that was a stumbling block. 'Twas something Elisabeth and I never did, and I regret it." Iain shrugged and shook his head. "I have enough years in me that it is not the obstacle it might have been for a younger man."

"That is what I thought when I asked her," Rob said.

He raised a brow at Iain's glare. "When things looked hopeless with Anice, I asked Robena to marry me and return to Dunbarton to live, too," he explained. "We were friends. We were lovers. I thought marriage would work between us, and that she would see the benefits to such an arrangement." Rob glanced over and smiled at Iain, but the expression on his friend's face was not one of mirth. He was not jesting about this. "Ye see how successful I was in gaining her hand in marriage."

Since Rob and Anice had been married for nigh on five years, Iain understood it had been in the past. That fact did not prevent a fire of jealousy from flaring within him as Iain thought of that possibility now. Somehow, Robena plying her trade with men for coin did not bother him as much as it would if she loved them. Daft, aye. Mad, even, but that was how he felt about it.

"Ye were in love with Anice. Ye would not have married Robena."

Rob shrugged then and stood away from the fence.

Nodding at the men who entered the yard and the others making their way to and from the keep, it was clear that the more personal part of this discussion was over.

"Think carefully, my friend," Rob warned. "If ye are serious about this offer, I will back ye in it."

"I am, Rob," Iain said.

"Do not hurt her, Iain. Others have. I have. But not again."

Loud voices drew their attention, and he watched as Struan came out of the keep with Anice following. They were having some argument that he did not wish to be witness to, and, from the way Rob's focus moved to them, it was one in which Rob needed to be involved.

"I will see you at supper," Rob said, walking past Iain and towards the only woman who truly mattered to his friend.

"Nay. I'll be in the village for a few days."

His words brought Rob to a complete stop there.

Turning back, he canted his head, staring at Iain.

"Do ye ken what yer doing, Iain? Have a care there."

Then Rob strode off, his pace picking up as the argument or discussion did, and Iain made a quick escape back to the village. If he was lucky, she would still be warm and sleepy on the pallet and he could slide back in next to her and enjoy the morning in her arms.

Chapter 7

Robena woke as Iain left. No matter his best efforts not to wake her, she missed his warmth as soon as he climbed from the pallet. It took a few minutes to dress and shake out and fold up the bedcovers. She shivered as she stepped out the back door of the cottage to bring in a bucket of water she'd left there. The icy layer was thicker than the last one, so she knew that the weather outside had taken a wintry turn. 'Twould not be long before snow covered the village and Dunnedin sank into the clutches of winter.

She inhaled the cold and clear morning air before ducking back inside and closing the door against the chill. Another shiver wracked her, and she grabbed up a blanket and wrapped it around her shoulders. A few minutes' effort and she had the fire burning brighter. When it began to warm, she dropped the blanket and went about the tasks that began the day for her. His absence confused her.

Was he gone for the whole of the day? Glancing in the corner, she saw that his bag was still there and mostly undisturbed. Wondering on his plans would do her no good, so she put a pot on the hook over the growing fire and filled it with some of the water. She would make enough porridge so there was plenty for him if he did come back soon, and if he did not, she could eat it through the day or store it for the next morning.

The purposeful strides crunching over the frozen grass of the path to her cottage made her turn and wait as the visitor approached. The steps slowed and then stopped.

Very slowly and quietly, the latch of the door lifted and the door inched open. When Iain's face came into view, she smiled as he frowned.

"Damn!" he said as he entered quickly and pushed the door closed behind him. "I was hoping to find ye yet asleep under the covers." He rubbed his massive hands together and blew on them. "The air is much colder today. And it feels like snow is approaching."

"The water will be ready soon, and I will make some hot tea—a concoction that Moira favors—that will warm ye from the inside out," she offered.

Standing up after checking the not-boiling water, she pushed her hair out of her face and back over her shoulders. The silence alerted her first. He stood by the door, not moving now, just staring at her.

"Come here, lass," he said in a soft voice.

Robena walked to where he stood, and he opened his arms to her. Embracing her, he leaned his chin on her head and rubbed down over her back. She may have sighed aloud at the comfort of it. When he laughed, the rumble of it spreading out through his chest so she could feel it next to her face, she understood she had sighed loud enough for him to hear.

"I canna help it, Iain. Ye are a warm man on a cold morning," she admitted. When she would have stepped away, he held her close.

"I needed to speak to Rob," he said. "Or I would not have risked freezing my bollocks off outside."

"Dinna risk yer bollocks, Iain," she said, laughing then.

Now he let her free and she went over to the hearth. After moving the pot for the tea closer to the flames to warm, she went to get the crushed betony leaves from the shelves. He was behind her, reaching over her head to get the jar down for her.

Over the next short while, this give-and-take continued as he wordlessly helped her make the tea, stir the porridge, and ready the bowls and cups to break their fast. If truth be told, this was one of her most treasured things about the time they spent together. On mornings like this one, and the ones like this that they'd shared over the last five years, she could almost pretend that their life was something different than it was.

As they moved around each other, sharing gentle touches as they carried out the menial and usual tasks of the morning, Robena could almost let herself believe they were man and wife rather than a man and his whore.

The revelation of last night was nowhere to be found between them now. They fell back into the comfortable pattern that had developed during his longer visits, and the morning meal passed in companionable ease.

"I have been helping Moira out several mornings a week, Iain. Would ye like to come with me?" She watched as he considered her words. "Or we can stay here, if ye'd rather?"

"Although I did see Pol at the miller's, I have not seen her yet. Do ye think she would mind me stomping into her cottage?" He retrieved her cloak, dropped it on her shoulders, and then got his.

"Ye have to see her lasses. They seem to grow inches every week."

He met her gaze and she recognized the wariness there. As though he was worried over her reaction to bairns. 'Twas one reason she did not reveal the truth to very many people. They treated her differently once they knew. Now, though, Iain opened the door and waited for her to pass.

The walk to Moira's cottage, a much larger one that sat on the edge of the village, took a short time, but they may have been rushed along by the cold winds that swirled along the paths and roads. Winter was here, and as Iain had said, snow was coming soon. Iain reached out and took hold of her hand to steady her steps along the ground that was hardened and slippery from the frost.

Another moment that filled with a dreamlike feel of a normal life wove around her, just as their heated breaths spun over their heads before dissipating in the cold. Moira opened the door before they could knock, and bade them to come in. As always, the scents inside Moira's cottage rushed over Robena as she entered.

Racks of dried and drying herbs and plants hung over their heads, though Iain came close to knocking into them as he walked.

"Come in! Come in and warm yerselves," Moira said.

Iain leaned down to enter through the doorway that was shorter than him. "Move nearer the fire, where it is warm."

Iain released her hand and followed her across the cottage to the hearth. In the far corner sat large tables next to a hearth that dwarfed her own. Moira lived and worked here—blending and concocting brews and tisanes and poultices and more from the herbs and plants she grew in the large garden outside or sought in the countryside around the village. So accomplished was she as a healer that Moira was permitted to send to other villages and even a monastery for the ingredients she needed but did not or could not cultivate herself.

Over the last month or so, as the harvesting reached its peak, Moira had asked for Robena's help and Robena had gladly given it. Spending time working and learning at the woman's side fascinated her. Though only a few years separated her age from Moira's, the woman's knowledge and experience were vastly different. The woman never stopped moving, doing, and making, and Robena trailed behind or alongside her as she worked. In that time, she'd learned to make a decent tea with several different leaves, to properly bind up a mixture of herbs for cooking various stews and soups, and when to move certain drying plants away from the fire so they were not too brittle. Without thinking, she did that now, seeing the color of a few of them nearest the hearth and recognizing they were done.

"My thanks," Moira said. "I had not gotten to those yet." The woman used her skirt over her hand to pull a large pot away from the fire as she spoke. "Can ye feel the change in the air? Snow will be here within a day or two." Using the dipper, she filled two cups with a steaming brew and then offered it to her and Iain. "Here. This will warm ye."

Robena inhaled the aroma before sipping the liquid. Not the usual flavor, she glanced over her cup at Moira.

"Not betony?"

"Nay, nay," Moira said with an enigmatic smile. "Something different this time." The healer leaned her hips back against the edge of the nearest table and nodded at them.

"Iain, 'tis good to see ye. How do ye fare?"

"I am well," Iain said with a smile. God Almighty, but the man was handsome! And he was a puzzle to her even now, after five years of seeing to his needs.

As she watched, enjoying the hot tea and observing him, she was struck by the way he was so unperturbed, no matter to whom he spoke. Robena had seen him with Struan when other nobles were present, and she'd watched him here in the village over the years since he began visiting Rob, and not once had he seemed ill at ease. He laughed easily, often, and well, as Moira told him about her lasses and their antics.

What shocked her, though, was when he put his cup down, still in conversation with Moira, and lifted

Robena's cloak from her shoulders and tossed it on a bench. These small gestures, ones that existed between a man and a woman, threatened her control. She could almost believe …

"Robena?" She blinked and found the two staring at her. "Do ye mind, then?" he asked.

"Mind?"

"I am going to Pol's smithy to lend a hand there," he explained. He needed not ask her permission for anything, and yet he was doing just that.

"Ye ken how men are, Robena," Moira said with a laugh. "Too much time listening to the tales of women and they break out in hives," she teased.

"If ye wish, Iain," she said, nodding. "Of course. Do as ye want."

His gaze narrowed as though studying her, and the corner of his appealing mouth lifted, and he smiled. He took but a step towards the door before coming back to stand in front of her. The kiss, quick and sweet, surprised her. He was out the door before she could take a breath.

"Well then," Moira whispered as she moved along the table.

"What do ye mean by that?" she asked, touching her fingers to her lips and then dropping her hand as Moira met her gaze.

"Things are going well between the two of ye?" The words were both a statement and a question.

"Iain is a pleasant man," she said. The description sounded tepid even to her ears, and Moira's nod and raised brow informed Robena that her attempt to minimize his action was unsuccessful. "He is no burden to serve."

"Of all the ways to describe that man," Moira began, "pleasant is not the word I would use." Moira walked towards her now, and Robena was tempted to step away.

"Something is different this time," she said. "Should he not be in the keep or with Rob?"

"He is avoiding Struan," Robena explained. "The laird is attempting to match his cousin Gunna and Iain."

"Ah, I ken no man who would want to marry that one," Moira said. She took Robena's cup and filled it once more. "So, he runs to yer side."

"He runs away from Struan," she corrected. She did not want Moira making assumptions that were not true. "And he pays me well enough that he can run to my side or my bed or away from them as he pleases." She must keep things in their places. She must not look at him as anything but a customer—a man who was paying very well for her time and attentions. He was only that.

"Just so."

Two words, uttered quietly, and yet they challenged so much. She looked away, pretending to examine the bunches of herbs above them, so she would not see understanding in Moira's very clear, very knowing eyes. The woman was not only a gifted healer, but also a gifted seer. Stories of her otherworldly insight were whispered through the clan. Though she'd never witnessed such a thing, Robena could easily believe it of the woman.

Moira let it go, handing her a basket of dried herbs and such, and Robena began following Moira's instructions. When she reached the bottom of the basket and a tidy pile lay next to it, Robena finally said what was on her mind.

"He kens, Moira."

"What does he ken?"

"All of it, I think," she said, staring at the flames in the hearth. "I told him I couldna bear children, and then he sought out Rob this morn." She shrugged. "From the look in his eyes, the pity there, he kens all of it."

"Ye think he pities ye, Robena? When ye look in his eyes, that's what ye see there?" Moira asked. The woman stood in front of her, waiting for Robena to look at her. Robena glanced up and nodded.

"Aye."

"Then ye do not ken men as I would think a woman who has whored as long as ye have would."

Robena gasped, for Moira had never called her that. No matter what the woman had seen or heard, or what injuries she had tended, Moira had never called her a whore.

"That man has a care for ye. That man looks on ye, not with pity, but with wanting and needing and caring."

"Nay." Robena shook her head, trying to deny it to herself, too. "Nay. He canna." She clasped her hands together, feeling the thing that kept her in control, the line that separated those long-ago dreams from the life she lived, start to weaken. "I am just his whore."

"Ye are trying to fool yerself, Robena. A man cares not if his whore canna have bairns or how it happened. He only worries if she canna give him pleasure or if he can take it on her."

"Ye dinna understand, Moira," she said.

What Moira said and the woman's way of seeing things were dangerous. If she allowed that Iain was more than just a man who paid for her, it would open up the dark, desperate need within her for more. More than lying beneath a man. More than waiting for him to arrive and waiting for him to leave.

"I think I do," Moira whispered as she took Robena's hands in her own. "Ye have made a place for yerself here for years and not permitted yerself to want or need more. But 'tis not working, is it?"

Whatever she would have said, however she would have denied Moira's words of truth, was stopped by the door bursting open. Pol was carrying Jean in his arms. She babbled as she wrapped her father's hair around her fingers. It was the sight of Iain carrying the younger one, Caitlin, in his arms and smiling at her, that tore Robena apart.

"They are hungry…again!" Pol said as he put his daughter down and took the other from Iain. "And ready to come home," he explained. He strode to Moira and kissed her. "As I am, but I have too many tasks to see to."

When Iain's gaze met hers, Robena feared for everything. Her well-ordered life, her identity, and her beliefs were all in grave danger from this man. Overwhelmed by fear, she simply walked out and away from them. From him.

"Robena?" She heard his voice but did not stop.

"Lass?"

She ran then, realizing for the first time that he was

the only man who would call his whore 'lass'. Heedless of her direction, she stumbled along the paths and into the woods, just knowing she needed to be away. When she stopped, her sides ached from the exertion and her lungs burned from the coldness of the air she breathed. Leaning over, hands on her thighs, she dragged in deep breaths. It took minutes or longer for her to become aware of the place to which she'd run.

This was the place where her life had been taken from her. All it took was one glance at the large rock in this clearing to know.

They'd dragged her here from her cottage, for there was not enough room for all of them there. Here, they could do as they wanted, far enough from the nearest cottages so that they did not draw attention. And they had done as they wanted, with a brutality she'd never experienced or seen. Having several men at once was something she'd done before, but then, the goal of those men had been pleasure, and lots of it. That night, the night of Alesander and Anice's wedding, those men had not desired pleasure. They'd wanted to hurt her and carry out some need of their leader for retribution.

And she had gotten both in full measure, as Struan's son had planned. It had gone on for hours before they'd dragged her back and left her in front of her cottage, torn and beaten and bleeding and…damaged. After that night, she'd changed too, for she understood there was nothing else for her but the life of a whore.

With a final look around, she accepted the memories for what they were now—a reminder that her path remained clear. She might fill her empty hours with interests and pursuits, but she was what she would always be—a whore. The crunching behind her made her turn quickly.

Iain stood there, staring at her.

Did he know the details of what had happened? Had Moira revealed more to him than Rob? Robena knew Rob felt guilty over what had happened to her and blamed himself somehow. His half-brother was the guilty one, though, and the only one to blame. And every day, God forgive her, she prayed that he yet burned in hell.

"I thought ye might need this if ye plan to stay outside," he said quietly as he held out her cloak. He was not wearing his. When she did not speak or move, he continued. "Moira said she would appreciate yer help for a few hours, if ye can spare it."

The urge to run gathered within her. It would be the right thing to do now. Run away from this man who threatened everything she had settled in her life. Run away from the growing need within her for more. But if she did, who would she be? Could she continue to simply whore for a living? Would she ever be able to ignore the longing for a family and a man of her own? Taking a breath, she gathered herself back in and gained control over the dangerous desires and nodded to him.

"With yer permission, I will," she said, once more the whore whose customer decided what she could or would do with her time.

Something flashed in his gaze, before he gave his permission with a curt nod. He waited there as she passed, handing her the cloak, which she tossed over her own shoulders as she walked by him.

It was simpler this way. To be what she knew she was, rather than to want something she could not have. By the time she reached Moira's cottage, the despair had been pushed back to where it belonged, and she was the same old Robena that everyone expected her to be.

Iain had watched her for some time before she came back to herself from whatever she was remembering or seeing here. Her eyes were haunted, and she shivered several times, though he doubted the cold was what caused it. As he waited, he realized what this place must be.

Moira must have known, for she'd given him directions on how to get here, explaining that Robena often found her way here. But why? Why return to the place where such a monstrous thing had happened? He shifted his weight and crushed some branches on the ground there, drawing her gaze.

For a moment, he wanted to look away from the anguish and horror he saw there, but Iain would not. He would not pity or lessen what she had survived by giving her anything but his strength. He'd trained men and seen them near their breaking point. Kindness was the last thing they needed, and it was the last thing she needed right now.

He told her what Moira had said and held out her cloak, fighting the urge to take her in his arms and banish whatever demons haunted her now. Iain forced his hands to his side as she took her cloak and walked away.

The cold surrounded him, but it did not stop his blood from boiling in his veins. If he could dig up Alesander MacKendimen and kill him again, slowly and painfully, he would. If he could find out the names of the men who had attacked Robena on his behalf and torture them as they'd tortured her, he would. The scream that bubbled up from inside him and echoed out over this clearing and through the woods was filled with his fury and frustration that he could do neither.

He could do nothing to avenge the wrong to this woman. He could do nothing to punish those responsible. Iain understood that Rob would have done it if he could have. Now he truly comprehended Rob's dilemma in this.

Iain would do the same thing his friend had done—give her a choice—and not try to bend her to his will or force her to accept him. He would indeed offer her marriage as one of the options, but the other, the much harder one for him, would be to change nothing between them. It would be a struggle to let a woman like her—a vibrant, intelligent, witty, loving woman—get away, but if that was what she truly wanted, he would let her go.

Iain loved her enough to do just that.

Instead of following her back to Moira's, he headed to the smithy to work out some of the fruitless anger he felt on her behalf. Pol took one look at him and put him to work without another word. After several hours of lifting and carrying and helping the much-younger blacksmith in his labors, Iain was exhausted and hungry and appeased. Well, as appeased as a man could be when he wanted to kill an already-dead man and his accomplices. Wearing himself out this way would have to do.

By the time they returned to Moira and Pol's home, all he wanted was to have Robena to himself, but there was a hot meal to be shared. Then several more hours of good conversation before she seemed ready to leave. As they walked back to her cottage, the snow began to fall.

The day of Christ's Mass was approaching more quickly than he'd realized. A few more days and he would have to return to the keep, for Struan would take it as a personal insult if he chose to remain with Robena and not celebrate the holyday with the laird's family.

That night, in the darkest hours, she initiated their coupling. He was content to hold her, but Robena began to touch and caress him, and then she climbed over him and slid down his readied cock in silence. Iain let her have her way, let her do as she wished, until she gained the satisfaction she seemed to need in the way she needed it. 'Twas as though she needed to prove to herself that she could after the terrible memories she'd faced this day.

The next days and nights fell back into their accustomed pattern. It surprised him at first, but Iain recognized that she was terrified of doing anything with him but that with which she was familiar. 'Twas as though revisiting the place where her life had been irreparably changed had also reminded her of her established role here. Did she fear doing anything else but the familiar?

She'd never sought out Moira, but she helped if someone asked her. She'd placed herself at his disposal, never far from his side when he needed or wanted her. At times, the fury inside him flared, and he went off to pound on metal with Pol until it ebbed back to a level he could control.

When the morning came for him to leave her and return to the keep for a few days, Iain decided it was time. Time to ask her. Time to hope she had the courage to accept.

Chapter 8

Robena watched as he dressed.

Struan had sent word that Iain was expected at the keep for the next few days while the laird and those closest to him observed the festivities surrounding Christ's Mass. There would be a feast the night before, this night, and then a solemn mass prayed in the chapel in the morning.

Since the day when Iain had found her in the place of her disgrace, she'd managed to regain her control and set things aright. He'd seemed to fall back into the usual pace of his previous visits, and so they spent their days here or walking in the village, visiting those he knew. Sometimes he would give her a look and then disappear for some time, only to return smelling of the smithy. It had been better when he did not know her truth, but it all seemed to be settling back as it should between them.

Now, though, he kept glancing at her in a strange way as he pulled his shirt on and placed the plaid around his waist. Part of her wanted to ask what was in his mind, but the other part knew not to do so. It was begging trouble to come to her door, and she knew it. Iain lifted his cloak from the peg at the door and turned to her. Why did dread fill her as he dropped the cloak and strode to her?

His mouth was hot and possessive then, more like the first time he'd kissed her when he arrived here. Did he wish to tup before he left? He pulled his head back and searched her face before meeting her gaze.

"I have something I want ye to think on while I am at the keep," he whispered. He kissed her again and then lifted his mouth from hers. "When I leave here after Hogmanay, I want ye to come with me."

"Come with ye, Iain? Where do ye wish to go?" She'd not gone too far from this village in all her years.

"I want ye to return to Dunbarton with me, lass," he said.

Did he want her as his leman? Would his nephew permit such a thing when they all knew she'd been a MacKendimen whore for years?

"I dinna understand, Iain. How can I go there with ye?" she asked.

His stare, the intensity in his gaze, and the way he held her close all warned her before he spoke that this was serious. If he had not been holding her, she would have fallen at his reply.

"I want ye as my wife, Robena. I want ye to marry me."

Of all the things that anyone could ever have said to her, those words had never been a possibility. That a man, any man, but especially a man with connections to nobility and power, would ask her such a thing. She studied his face now, looking for signs that he was jesting.

"I mean it, lass. I wish to marry ye."

Robena pushed out of his embrace and walked to the other side of the cottage, smoothing her hands over her gown. This was madness, plain and simple. He could not mean to marry her. She glanced at his face to see truth there—he did.

"I thank ye for honoring me so, Iain," she began. Twisting her hands together, she smiled, or tried to, to soften her words. "That is just not possible."

"Why not?" he asked. He took a step towards her and, God forgive her, she backed a step away. He stopped then and crossed his arms over his chest, as she'd seen him do hundreds of times. Was he asking her to explain why this could not be?

"Are ye daft then, Iain? Ye are kin to The MacKillop and I am a MacKendimen whore."

"Ye whore for a living, Robena. 'Tis not who ye are."

"Iain, I am a whore," she said. He must stop this madness.

"And if ye married me, ye'd be my wife. What difference is that?"

"Iain, again, I am honored beyond measure, but there is no reason for ye to even ask this."

"I want ye, Robena. I want ye with me always. I love ye, lass."

She lost her breath at his words. The words she had craved, the ones she'd dreamt of hearing spoken to her for so many years. Not now though. Not now.

"There is no place for love between a man and the whore he pays."

He stood to his full height then and bristled like a wild animal about to charge. But even now, as she insulted his offer and refused him, she did not fear him physically. As he took a step towards her, she fought the urge to run. He might not hurt her body, but this could tear her heart and soul apart. A few long strides put him right in front of her.

"Tell me ye dinna feel something for me, lass." When she would have replied, he shook his head. "Dinna lie to me and use that excuse about a man and his whore. I am asking ye now, man to woman, is there nothing else between us but the passion we share in yer bed?"

She was more practiced at lying than she was at giving a voice to the truth. A whore lied about what she felt. About what she wanted. About what she thought. It protected her and allowed her to retain something of her own self when others used her body for their purposes.

She'd lived those lies and meant those lies, but now, looking at this man, she was tempted not to.

Experience and cold, hard practicality won out.

"My bed, Iain? We have fucked on the floor, against the wall and the door and out in the grass behind the cottage." She forced a whore's smile onto her face then. "We have shared so much passion and pleasure. Is that what ye mean?" His face grew red and she could feel his anger pouring off him in waves.

"I have surprised ye, I ken. I think there is more here,

more between us, no matter yer words now." He walked away and Robena clenched her hands into fists, fighting the need to call out to him. "I want ye to think on this while I am at the keep these next days."

Robena looked away then, not able to watch him, and the loud slamming of the door spoke of his departure. She stood there in the silence, trying to accept that this was her life. No matter his kind words or his bold offer, there could be nothing more than pleasure and desire between them.

She did not move for a long time, battling her own heart's desire to run after him. The need to follow him pushed her a few stumbling steps toward the door, but she fell to her knees rather than allow herself to weaken in her resolve.

She would never accept his offer, for it would put him in a terrible situation between his kin and his duties to his clan. She would never be accepted by any of them, and it would take no time at all before he blamed her for that.

The laugh that escaped her was a sad one. For just one single moment then, she allowed herself to think he meant it, that it could be possible. It took little time at all to ken that no matter how Rob had managed to smooth things out for her in the past, this was not possible.

Robena climbed to her feet then and walked to the pallet. She stared at it, remembering everything that they shared. Nay, he was correct, there was something more between them. And it was something that would make her refuse his offer and keep them as they were and should be—a man and his whore.

More than that could simply never be.
She loved him too much to ever allow it.

Iain sat at the table and watched the festivities with a blind eye. All around him people ate and drank. The food tasted like dirt in his mouth. The wine, the laird's finest he'd been told, could have been cow's piss for all he cared.

He went through the expected motions of meeting and greeting Struan's visitors and being pleasant to his still-present cousin. Rob watched him and Iain knew his friend could not figure out the cause of his aloofness. But Iain did not wish to talk of it to anyone.

He'd misjudged Robena and misjudged her badly.

Now he'd scared her. He'd read the fear in her eyes—like a wild animal caught in the snare and searching for a way, any way, to escape. He did not fool himself into believing her words about not caring for him outside of their bedplay. But, like a trapped creature, she had struck out and tried to keep him at a distance.

"Ye are deep in thought, my friend," Rob said as he leaned over from Iain's right. "What did ye do wrong?"

"Why do ye blame me?" he asked.

"Come now, Iain. Ye were married long enough to ken that it is always our fault, no matter what was done or not done. No matter what we said or did not say."

"I am so glad that ye learned that in only five years of marriage, husband." Anice leaned past Rob and smiled.

Placing her hand on Rob's, she continued, "'Twill make the next decade or two so much easier for me." Rob leaned his head back and laughed.

Good God, but they were in love. It hurt Iain to watch it playing out so clearly before him.

"So, again, I ask ye—what did ye do?"

Iain took another mouthful of the wine, finishing the cup, and held it up for a servant to fill once more. 'Twas his fourth? Nay, fifth cup. But what difference did it make? No matter how much he drank, he could not rid himself of the memory of the haunted expression in her eyes when he'd left. He put the cup down, knowing it would not help him.

"Anice." He leaned forward and looked past Rob to the man's wife. "Would ye send someone to look in on Robena on the morrow?" He'd been back here for two days now, and he'd wanted nothing so much as to return to the village. But Struan had put obstacles and requests in his way that made certain he had not left the keep.

"On the morrow?" Anice asked, glancing at her husband first and then at him. "Is aught wrong?" When Rob turned now to him and shrugged, Iain knew he would have to tell her.

"I asked her to marry me."

Anice gasped so hard she sucked in a large amount of air and then choked on it. Iain watched as the coughing fit went on for several moments before she was able to stop.

"Ye what?" She yelled the question so loudly that everyone at table and below stopped and stared. His own mouth was probably agape, too. She stood then, forcing him and all the men present to stand, as she pointed towards the chamber above. "I would speak with ye in my solar," she said.

Pushing back, she left the table, not waiting on either Rob or Iain to follow. She just knew they would. Glancing around as he waited on Rob, he saw sympathy in varying levels in the gazes of the men who watched. He may have staggered a step or two before Rob took hold of his arm and led him up the stairs and into Anice's chamber. The lady, who only came up to her husband's chest, sat in her chair, tapping her foot on the stone floor.

"Tell me what ye have done, Iain." Her words were calmer than he thought they'd be. As he looked at the lady, he realized that Robena could have no better protector than her.

"I asked her to marry me, Anice. Plain and simple," he explained.

"Nothing men do is ever simple," she muttered.

"Anice, I kenned he was going to do this," Rob said. "I did not think it such a bad thing for Robena."

The lady, always so gentle and kind, looked as though she was going to kill someone. For a moment, he thought her husband would be the target, but when she turned her gaze on him, Iain thought again.

"I love the lass, Anice." Sometimes, the truth was the best defense, and it seemed to soften the lady's resistance.

"Does she ken that, Iain?"

"Aye, I told her. But she doesna believe it. She doesna

believe she can be loved or can live a different life than the one she has."

"And if she refuses yer offer? What will ye do then?"

Anice watched him closely while her own husband stood there at her side. Aye, Robena could have no better people watching out for her than these two.

Unless it was him.

"I have given her the chance to think on it. Then I will make my decision."

"Can ye stand by if she declines and remains here as a…as she is?"

A whore. The lady would not speak the word, but they all understood. If Robena turned him down, she would remain here, making a living by providing pleasure to other men. Could he truly leave her here knowing that?

If he loved her, if he loved her enough, then …

"Aye. If it is her wish to remain here, then so be it. I just want her to have enough time to consider it." He ran his hands through his hair and shook his head. "I did not like leaving her there alone, but Struan will not allow her here."

"What?" Anice stood then. "I have invited her here. I have made certain she is welcome."

"And Struan has warned her not to come. 'Tis his right as laird," he explained to a person who understood her father-by-marriage better than anyone else did.

"That explains much. I wish she had spoken of this to me."

"She seems to understand her place and accept it more than any of us do," Rob said.

And that was the heart of the matter. The woman he loved accepted her place. She understood the boundaries of her life and had discovered a way to exist within them. Was that how she survived? Knowing the expectations and keeping to them?

He did not want to believe that she was happy living within those limitations. He took her recent exploration into helping the midwife and learning from Moira as a sign of some unhappiness or some unfulfilled need within her. As much as he thought she would be happy as his wife, mayhap not even loving her gave him the right to expect it of her.

"Just make certain she is well," Iain said.

Turning away, he left the solar and made his way back to the chamber assigned to him.

He was a fool, and nothing was worse than an old fool.

He was no better than anyone else who tried to control her or bend her to his will. Worse, he was a liar as much as she was. Though he'd claimed he would allow her to do as she chose in this, in truth there would be no way he could stand by and let another man touch her. Not now.

Not again.

Good Christ, but he'd gotten himself into a quandary here. He'd thought he would come in, offer to take her away, and she would jump into his arms and be happy. He laughed then. Not Robena. She was strong enough to live life, even if she did not realize that it was that inner strength that kept her going.

He would go to see her on the morrow. He would say… something… that would ease his way and give her leave to ignore his offer. Not that he wanted her to refuse him. He prayed with every part of his heart and soul that she would accept it and him, but whatever happened, he would not make things worse. Well, not worse for her.

The amount of wine he'd had dragged him into a restless sleep, and he tossed and turned all night. He would wake and reach out for Robena, only to remember that he did not share her bed this night. And he did not like it.

The morning dawned cold and crisp, and he struggled to make it down to the hall to break his fast. Filled with many like him who had overindulged during the Christmas feast and festivities the nights and days before, Iain noticed that a good number of those did not seek out more ale this morn. Rather, dry crusts of bread seemed to be the only thing their thick heads, churning bellies, and painful megrims would tolerate. Mayhap now, with a clearer though more painful head than he'd had at last night's feast, he could sort out what to do about Robena.

Aye, he should have discussed his plan with another woman instead of relying on Rob. Now all he could do was try to make it right. A servant approached and said that the lady wished to see him in the kitchens, so Iain followed the lad back through the corridors to where the lady waited. Anice worked tirelessly, so it should not have surprised him that she'd already sent someone to the village as he'd asked. From the grave expression on her face, Iain did not know what to think.

"Lady?" he said, nodding as she waved off the servant.

"What is the matter?"

"I sent someone to see to Robena as you asked me to do," she said. She glanced around her before turning her gaze to him. "She is well."

"Well? That is good."

"The rope is gone from her gate."

Iain could not think. He could not believe it. He understood what that meant, but it could not be.

He was not certain if the lady had anything else to say or not, for he was walking out of the kitchen towards the stable before he even thought of a plan. His mind was empty as he rode down to the village and stopped in front of her cottage. The rope was indeed gone, and worse, he heard voices inside. Laughing voices. A man and Robena. Iain lifted the latch and walked in without knocking.

The only thing that kept the man alive was that Iain understood what was happening here. He knew that fear was driving her actions and that she was striking out in reaction. His experience training men taught him that, so he held himself in check. Well, all that and the fact that killing an unarmed man in the MacKendimen village would not go over well. The man pulled out of Robena's embrace at his entrance and backed away as he looked at Iain's face.

"Have ye started?" he asked, pushing the words out through his clenched jaws. Iain wanted to thrash the man to a bloody mess, but he forced himself to remember what this was really about. "Get out." He said the last words quietly, meeting Robena's gaze as she flinched.

Though he did not wish to pay heed to the man involved, that one scurried around the cottage, gathering whatever belongings he'd brought, and ran out the door. Her chest heaved as she watched him now, drawing in shallow, panting breaths of …

Fear.

Fear drove her. Fear of the unknown. Fear of him.

"What do ye think ye are doing, Robena?" he asked, moving away from the doorway so she would not feel trapped. He crossed the cottage and sat on a stool next to the table. Sitting down, he would be less threatening than standing and towering over her.

"I did not expect ye back, so I thought to…" She paused, and he watched as she swallowed.

"Are ye trying to see if ye can whore again now that ye ken that I love ye?" He shrugged. "Well, can ye?"

When she did not answer, he reached inside the sporran he wore and grabbed a handful of coins. Tossing them on the table before him, he nodded at them.

"There. Ye have been paid for yer time, up to now." He reached in again, grabbing more and throwing them onto the pile. "And until I leave for Dunbarton." He added another handful. "And for a long time after I am gone." The amount on the table was more than she would earn in months, if not an entire year. "Now, 'tis up to ye if ye want to sell the pleasure ye give for coin."

"Iain," she whispered. "Do not do this." That haunted expression was back, and it tore his heart out of his chest.

"Do not misunderstand this, my love. Ye think ye are only a whore, and I ken ye are more than that. Moira kens that ye are. As does Daracha. As do Margaret and Conran. Lady Anice and Robbie. So many others here see and value the woman ye are, lass, even if all ye see is the whore who earns her way on her back."

"I have only been the whore, Iain. 'Tis all I ken. All my mother was before me." Her words revealed to him that it was more than that she was clinging to what she knew. There was doubt there, doubt that she was only that which she proclaimed herself. And doubt helped him.

"That"—he nodded at the coins— "gives ye a long time to think on what ye wish yer life to be like, lass. If ye will not accept my offer, at least ye can consider yer path. Make no mistake though, I pray ye will accept mine."

He stood then and walked to her. Sliding his hands into her hair, he brought her to him and kissed her. She covered his hands with hers and opened her mouth to him. He tasted her deeply, tasted the saltiness of her tears and the warmth of the woman she was. Lifting his lips from hers, he smiled and let her go.

The hardest thing he'd ever done in his life to this day was to watch his beloved Elisabeth die. Now, he had to walk away and let Robena go. A few paces to the door was all he needed take, and Iain struggled to find the strength.

She must choose him also if they were to find happiness together. With each step, he prayed that she would stop him. He waited for one word. Even a sound. He reached the door and the silence was a chasm between them now.

Without looking back, Iain walked out.

Chapter 9

Winter came in earnest over the days before Hogmanay. Each day brought a few more inches until a thick blanket covered all of Dunnedin. It could have been worse, though, for storms could move through the mountains and glens with vicious winds and dangerous amounts of snow and hail. This year seemed to want to slide away quietly and give way to the new one without a struggle. Robena thought that Iain's departure from her cottage would give her some peace, but that did not happen. Over the next days, days more of darkness than light, she was summoned to help at two more births, and Moira sought her out to finish the important tasks of storing enough of her supplies to see them through until spring.

She did not have to ask if Iain had left, for she saw him several times in the village. He would look at her for a few moments before smiling at her and moving on to whatever task he carried out. One day Moira mentioned he'd been working with Pol, and Robena had to stop herself from going to see him there. Iain did not approach her and did not attempt to speak to her after that day, and she was glad of it.

Or so she told herself, every hour of every day that passed. Mayhap she would believe it by the time he went back home. Of course, she did not have to ask about him, for in the days leading up to the end of the year, every other person they knew in the village, and many from the keep, spoke their minds on the matter.

From the cook who came to Moira's for some ingredient needed for supper, to the midwife, to the miller's wife, and even Lady Anice herself, everyone seemed more than willing to meddle in something that should have been a private matter between just the two of them.

She'd not spoken to anyone of his offer apurpose, wishing not to insult the man who'd done her such a great honor. Somehow, though, everyone seemed to know, and felt free to speak of it to her. Moira made her opinion known in a few well-chosen, well-timed words of advice that made Pol suggest she heed her own counsel. 'Twould seem that the healer and blacksmith were no closer to marrying this year than the last.

Even Margaret's widowed sister-by-marriage spoke highly of Iain when Robena accompanied Daracha to see to the new bairn and his mother. When she thought on it, no matter which woman she encountered in the village, they all seemed to offer their unsolicited thoughts and opinions on the benefits of marrying Iain.

Lady Anice turned out to be worst, though, for she spoke about every possible other subject *save for* the man during their chance meetings. By the time the lady went on her way, Robena almost begged for news of him.

As the last night of the year began, Robena understood that he'd been right. She lived in fear. She existed as she was because she knew her way in life as she lived—a whore. The recent bout of hopelessness that seemed to take hold of her confirmed his words. Letting out a soft sigh, she stared into the fire burning in the hearth, and knew that she could not find a way to leave the fear or bleakness behind.

Worse, although she truly did not wish to admit this even to herself, she missed him terribly. Missed his smile and his way of teasing her. And his touches and caresses. The way he saw to her needs before his own. The talks and walks they shared.

She missed his love. A love she could never claim.

Her love for him would not allow her to enter into a relationship that would bring him nothing but sorrow, separation from his kin, and humiliation. For his clan would never allow such a marriage to stand, even if he were too softhearted to make it, and he would be forced to choose one over the other.

She would accept his gift, the coins he'd left for her with apparently no intention of getting his money's worth, and decide her path once he was gone from Dunnedin. Hopefully by the time he returned in the summer, as was his custom, he would forgive her for disappointing and refusing him.

Tears threatened once more as Robena lit the lantern and hung it outside her door. 'Twas an old tradition, but one the villagers observed each year on Hogmanay. A dark-haired man entering first predicted good luck, and if he carried bread or peat, or better still *uisge-beatha,* prosperity would be hers in the coming year. A fair-haired man told of misery and ill-fortune, and so they were to be avoided or shunned if they did knock. By now, most of the villagers with blond or red hair were safely kept in their cottages so they did not tempt the fates and bring down bad tidings for the year.

Too hollowed out by the last days and their emotional toll, she'd not made arrangements for the "first footing." Whoever entered through her door after midnight this night would foretell her fortune in the coming year, and she would have to accept whomever knocked this night.

Mayhap Moira would send Pol to her door to ensure her good fortune? Thinking on the heavy bag of coins hidden under her pallet, Robena did not need wealth. But inviting the fates' blessings would not be a bad thing.

So, as the hours passed, she waited for the sounds of the villagers making their way from cottage to cottage.

"Where are ye going now?" Rob asked.

"Where do ye think? To the damned village," Iain said.

He wrapped the thick cloak around his shoulders and grabbed up the chunk of bread he'd kept from supper, shoving it into a pocket sewn inside. Iain had reached the end of his patience.

Age and experience had given him a full measure of that quality, but even he had limits. He'd thought he could force her hand. Then he'd thought he could let her go. Now, as the year ended, Iain knew he could do nothing but take her on her own terms.

"I want her, Rob. If I have to, I will take her however she wishes. If she will marry me or not. I cannot lose her."

If she wanted to continue as she was, then he would have to find a way to accept even that. He would do what he must to keep her in his life or to remain in hers. That did not mean he would stop trying to convince her to marry him, but he could not lose her.

"'Tis about bloody time," Rob muttered.

"What?" Iain turned and faced his friend.

"Anice thought ye would have relented by now, but my guess was on the morrow."

"Ye have been betting on me? On us?" Iain looked at him, shocked by this revelation. Rob just reached over and slapped Iain's back, hard enough to make him stumble.

"Everyone has. Those in the village and those here in the keep," Rob said with a laugh. "The only one not involved is Struan. He is yet convinced his cousin Gunna has a chance of catching ye."

Iain shuddered then, at the thought of the poor man who would marry such a woman as Gunna. Rob gave him a shove and Iain strode to the door.

"If ye wish to make an impressive entrance, ye need to be there before anyone else. Get ye gone, my friend!"

Rob nodded and Iain ran to the stables. The gates remained open this night, and the villagers were carrying lanterns along the paths to light the way of those dark-haired men who would foretell good fortune when they knocked. Iain made it down the road to her cottage without seeing anyone approaching her door. He jumped down to the ground before her gate and tied his horse there.

He did not see the young woman until she nearly knocked him over.

Grabbing hold of her shoulders, he managed to stay on his feet on the slippery path there and keep her upright as well. When she raised her head, he did not recognize *her*.

"Are ye well, mistress?" he asked, studying her face. Tears yet streamed down her young face, and she nodded as she pulled from his grasp.

"Ask her to have a care for him, sir," she whispered as she threw a glance over her shoulder towards Robena's cottage. "There is no one else I can turn to. No one I would trust with him," she said before she turned and ran away into the darkness between the roads and cottages there.

Iain watched for some sight of her, but he could not see her now. Only when he walked closer to the door did he see the bundle lying there on the ground. Robena opened her door and watched his approach. The faint cry echoed into the stillness of the night as the packet at her feet moved and shook.

"Iain? What is this?" She fell to her knees there and

picked up the wrapped bundle and realized what she held. "What in all that is holy…?"

"I dinna ken." Iain had a suspicion, and he walked back to the gate and peered into the shadows looking for the young woman. He shrugged. "She left him and ran off."

"Who?" Robena asked as she loosened the coverings and revealed a wee bairn inside the bundle.

"Take him inside," he urged. "He will catch his death of cold outside on a night like this."

Iain helped her to her feet and they went inside, closing the door against the cold. Robena placed the bairn on the table and loosened the woolen blankets, revealing a babe who could not be more than a few days old. The bairn's tiny wrinkled face eased for a moment before he let loose a strong and full cry. Just as quickly, Robena wrapped him back up, swaddling him with an expert hand and lifting the babe to her shoulder.

"Who would do such a thing, Iain?" she asked as she held the bairn close and patted his back. Iain watched as Robena shushed the wee thing and rocked it in her embrace and understood what had happened.

"She said to ask ye to have a care for him. That she could turn to no one else but ye, Robena." The dumbstruck expression on her face must have matched his own, for the implications were unbelievable.

"Someone left her bairn on my doorstep?"

Iain walked to her and gathered them both in his embrace. He kissed her then, hoping she realized the importance of this selfless gesture. In giving her son to

Robena, this young woman told her of her value. Of her worth. Of her abilities.

"Someone trusted ye to care for the child she could not keep." He kissed her then and wiped the tears she did not know she shed from her cheeks. "Will ye believe me now, my love? That others see in ye what ye cannot see in yerself? What I see in ye?"

Robena shook her head. He could see her struggle to accept this truth.

"Take my hand, Robena. Take my love. I ken ye are frightened, but surely ye will have the faith that others have in ye to try?"

The bairn let out a sleepy sigh and Robena stared at the rosebud mouth and thick thatch of dark hair on his head.

"Ye see, the fates sent ye a message this night. A dark-haired… male… was first over yer door for the new year. And in case that is not enough, I brought along bread," he said as he pulled the chunk out of his pocket. "Surely this is a sign that ye will have good fortune in the coming year."

He held his hand out then, hoping that she could take it.

Robena stared at his hand and the few steps between them and wondered if she would take hold of him. It would take less effort to reach for him than it would to resist, but something held her back.

Was he also correct about this being a sign? The bairn let out a burp and nestled against her chest then, settling down in her arms. He did not seem to care that she was a whore. His mother had not cared, for her words to Iain had made it clear that the woman knew who lived within, and who would see to her son. A stranger in need, who had sought out Robena's protection for her child; it touched her heart and gave her a glimmer of hope in an improbable future.

Could it be that she was resisting Iain and his offer for another reason?

Robena had not hidden away from the truths of her life and her unsuitability for him. She'd argued it and accepted it, but no one else seemed to. And she'd not kept anything secret from him—he knew her as few did, the good with the bad. She glanced at his outstretched hand before meeting his gaze.

Love filled his eyes.

In spite of what she did, in spite of her limitations, he loved her. And she knew that she loved him, deeply and without expectations. So, what did she need to do to accept his offer? Trust him. Trust that he understood what they would face. Trust that he would stand by her. Trust that his offer was an honest one.

Her throat tightened, even as her heart pounded in her chest. Though she might doubt herself and her worthiness, he never did. Gazing into his eyes, she knew in that moment that she trusted him. Trusted his word. Trusted his love.

How could she not trust herself, then?

"Aye, Iain. I cannot fight the fates…and ye," she said. She took his hand. His blue eyes flared at her words as he closed his fingers around hers and tugged her close, the bairn held between them. "If ye still want to marry me—us—I will."

"Oh aye, I would take ye as my wife, my love," he said.

Epilogue

The words they'd spoken that night were repeated a fortnight later before the MacKendimen priest, and Robena found herself married. Even now, hours after the ceremony, she could not stop staring at the gold band on her finger and at the man who she loved, and trusted, enough to take the biggest risk in her life. The villagers turned out to watch, even as those who'd lost their bets paid those who'd won. The only one who did not attend was the laird himself.

Iain had faced Struan's wrath when he'd returned to the keep and announced it to those gathered. He'd respected the laird's order that she should not enter the keep, so after informing him of the coming nuptials, Iain had gathered the rest of his belongings and moved to her cottage.

In the two weeks since Hogmanay, they'd searched for the bairn's mother to no avail. No one reported a missing woman or babe, so Robena decided to honor the poor woman's request and take care of her son. Iain seemed more than pleased at the gift that they'd been given, and the bairn truly was that. They had much yet to be settled, but they would do it together.

"What would ye have done if he'd had red hair?" she asked as she lifted the bairn to her shoulder and patted his back. As a loud burp bubbled out of wee Duncan, as they called him, Robena watched Iain's gaze and waited for his answer.

"I would have found another way to make ye see reason, my love. Red-haired or black, ye were not getting away." Iain leaned down over her as she sat near the fire, feeding the babe, and kissed her again. His hand on her head would have held her there for another kiss, but he pulled back when the door pushed open and a young man entered.

"Uncle," the man said in a furious voice.

"Nephew," Iain said in just the same tone, facing their visitor.

"I received word of a marriage. One ye entered into without my permission."

They'd known that Struan had sent a messenger to Dunbarton as soon as he'd learned of their plans. Only the snowy roads had kept anyone from arriving sooner. Robena now looked from one man to the other and saw the resemblance of kin. None other than James MacKillop, chieftain of the Clan MacKillop, stood in her cottage.

"I have done yer bidding, Jamie," Iain said, stepping aside so his laird could see her there. "As ye have asked me to do of late."

"Struan tells me ye married the village whore and

have taken in a foundling as well. What were ye thinking, uncle?"

Robena watched with a sense of awe as Iain grabbed the younger man by his throat, dragged him to the door and tossed him out. She stood and would have followed, but Iain waved her back.

"Keep the bairn warm," he whispered to her, before he walked outside and stood over his nephew.

She held wee Duncan close, but she did walk to the door and peered through a slight opening to watch her husband. She offered up a prayer of thanksgiving to the Almighty that she had come to her senses and accepted this man as husband. He stood proud and fearless over a man who could make his life, their life, a miserable hell or a happy one.

"I was thinking that ye wanted me to marry again. Robena brought gold and a son into our marriage, more than yer own wife did, Jamie." She noticed Iain did not say it was his own gold returned to him.

"Ye twist my words, uncle," Jamie said as he climbed to his feet and tried to assert his position as chief. "I had any number of acceptable brides for ye to choose from. Ye did not have to lower yerself to take a whore."

The quiet but swift punch knocked the man back to the ground. She was ready to go out and intercede, but she heard Rob call out a greeting to the younger man as he approached her cottage. Iain leaned down before Rob got close and shook his head at his nephew.

"I didna make a claim to be chieftain when my brother died because I believed ye would be a good leader for our clan. Now, dinna be an arse and make me regret that, Jamie."

There was silence then as Iain's nephew considered his words. When he got up without Iain knocking him back down, Robena thought they might have reached a tacit peace. Rob held out his hand in greeting, and Robena recognized his expression—the relief that he would not have to play the peacemaker after all.

"'Twill not be an easy thing to accept," Jamie said.

"I did not say 'twould be, but it is what it is."

Then Iain made the offer she had known he would. If this worked, it would make things easier for the others in their clan who would have rightful objections to their marriage and to her.

"I think 'tis time for me to step aside and let someone else—William, I think—take over as commander."

Jamie did not answer right away.

"And I think that I should oversee that southern estate for ye, my laird." Iain bowed his head and waited for his nephew's reaction. What Iain was offering was a practical solution for the uncomfortable situation that their marriage would cause.

She would not be accepted in the laird's household, but this would give his uncle a way to serve without causing constant problems. Anice had been the one to suggest it, and Rob agreed it was a pragmatic solution.

"I do need someone I can trust to protect our southern borders, Uncle," The MacKillop finally said. Robena let out the breath she'd been holding and smiled to herself.

"Come up to the keep. Anice has supper waiting on

ye," Rob offered, now that the storm had passed.

"Uncle? Do ye join us?" Jamie asked. Though he faced his uncle now, he stared over Iain's shoulder at her there in the doorway. This was the first of countless choices Iain would face because of her. She listened for his answer, not taking her gaze from The MacKillop's.

"I will be there shortly, Jamie. Rob, dinna wait on me to eat."

His nephew could have ordered his presence. But Jamie seemed to understand that there would be other times when he would need to do that, and he nodded now, looking back at his uncle. As soon as Jamie followed Rob away, Robena moved from behind the door, back nearer to the hearth.

"It worked," he said as he entered and walked to her side.

"Aye, 'tis a good plan, as long as ye are happy?" He would be giving up so much to have her at his side.

"Are ye with me, wife?" he asked in the deep voice that sent chills from her head to her toes. "If you are, then I am happy."

"I am, Iain." Unfortunately, there was no time to do anything about the desire that he called forth in her. "I will be waiting for ye, laddie," she promised. With a kiss, quick and hot and possessive, he strode to the door and lifted the latch. He waited until she met his gaze and smiled.

"And I will take off my boots for ye, lass."

Robena laughed as he pulled the door closed behind himself. She looked forward to the challenge he'd just offered her.

Even more than the fleeting moments of pleasure, she looked forward to a life with him—a future that she would never have dreamt was possible until Iain MacKillop made her believe it could happen.

Dear Readers –

Thanks so much for reading this story about an unlikely heroine and her unexpected hero. Robena and her fans have been asking for her Happily-Ever-After since she appeared in ONCE FORBIDDEN in 2002 and I finally got the chance to write it as part of an anthology called CHRISTMAS IN KILTS in 2017. Now, I have the chance to release her story by itself and am thrilled for it to take its place in my MacKendimen Clan series!

Other stories for the MacKendimens are swirling around and taking shape, so they're not finished yet!

Although this is a stand-alone story. if you're curious about where this story fits in the MacKendimen Clan series, here's the chronological order:

A Love Through Time

An archway in time…
A man in search of his future in the past…
A woman who holds the key…

Maggie Hobbs has had enough of controlling men in her life. Breaking up with her longtime boyfriend, she heads to Scotland for her summer vacation, hoping to put it all behind her—though she never dreams how far behind her it will go! During a stop at a clan ceilidh, Maggie meets the man who should be heir to the Clan MacKendimen—one whose father turned his back on his heritage for a new life in America. And then Fate steps in to throw her back to a time when men controlled everything!

Alex MacKendimen returns to his father's lands and discovers a life that could have been his. With the emptiness of his life staring back at him, he wished for another chance to find happiness and finds himself catapulted to the past – as he and a beautiful stranger face dangers together in medieval Scotland.

Thrown together and back to medieval Scotland by Fate, Maggie Hobbs and Alex MacKendimen must discover the reasons for their journey through time and face their greatest fears. Struggling to survive and to find a way home while falling in love, they must learn to trust each other more than they have ever trusted another. Will they make it out of the past or be forced to survive far away from everyone and all they know?

Once Forbidden

A Highland woman desperate for a hero...
A Highland warrior destined to save her...
Will love be enough to unite them forever?

Anice MacNab barely survived the brutal treatment of her wedding night, leaving her with a shattered life, body and soul. Now, the death of her husband forces her to flee another planned political alliance, seeking the help of the only man she trusts…

Robert Mathieson, raised as the son of a steward, discovers instead that he is the son of the MacKendimen laird. Denied recognition and refused his heritage, Robert still finds himself drawn into the intrigue surrounding Anice and wanting the one person he cannot have—his half-brother's wife.

Secrets of the past threaten the MacKendimen Clan and vows made will be broken as Robert and Anice claim the love, once forbidden, that could destroy many lives or could unite them forever.

A Highlander's Hope happens here!

A Matter of Time

*A man conceived in the past and living
  in the present…
A woman in need calling him back…
Where and when does his destiny lie?*

Current Day…

Douglas MacKendimen grew up listening to his parents' fantastical tales of their journey to the past and has never believed a word of it. Caught up in the stressful world of practicing medicine, the strange dreams during restless nights should not surprise him—but the woman calling to him does. The dreams intensify as he returns to Scotland for a family gathering.

Dunnedin, Scotland, 1370

Caitlin, daughter of the MacKendimen Clan healer, has even greater abilities than her mother and can heal with only her touch. Her power is growing as she tends to her kith and kin but is drawn to a man in her dreams. When he appears and saves her life, she believes they are meant to be together. The truth – that he is from the future and must return destroys all her hopes. She cannot abandon her clan to be with him and he must leave.

Secrets of the past and future threaten to destroy them as Douglas and Caitlin's love grows. When the fates are against them, it's just a matter of time before they will be forced to choose whether to follow their hearts' desires or to remain apart forever.

Meet Terri Brisbin

Award-winning and *USA Today* best-selling author **Terri Brisbin** is a mom, a wife, grandmom(!) and a dental hygienist who has sold 4 million copies of her historical and paranormal romance novels and novellas in more than 25 countries and 20 languages. Her current and upcoming historical and paranormal/fantasy romances are published by Harlequin Historicals and independently, too.

Visit her website for more info on Terri, her works and upcoming events.

Find all the links to her social media connections at:
www.linktr.ee/terribrisbin

TerriBrisbin.com

www.ingramcontent.com/pod-product-compliance
Lightning Source LLC
Chambersburg PA
CBHW060802210726
48292CB00013B/1733